Tongue, Tied and Other Short Plays

by

M. Thomas Cooper

SAMUEL FRENCH

FOUNDED 1830

NEW YORK HOLLYWOOD LONDON TORONTO

SAMUELFRENCH.COM

ISBN 978-0-573-66368-0   Printed in U.S.A.   #22321

IMPORTANT BILLING AND CREDIT REQUIREMENTS

TONGUE, TIED

Theatre: Artworks Enterprises

Actors:

TINA . . . . Rachel-Marie Wessel

TOM . . . . John R. Lewis

Director: Amanda Long

Date of Production: Ashland 10-minute play festival, 2006

Theatre: Actors Theatre of Louisvile

Actors:

TINA . . . . Emily Ackerman

TOM . . . . Stephen Plunkett

Director: Marc Masterson

Date of Production: Humana Festival, 2008

Theatre: City Theatre (Miami)

Actors:

TINA . . . . Elena Garcia

TOM . . . . Paul Tei

Director: Stuart Meltzer

Date of Production: Summer Shorts Festival, 2008

SKIRMISHES

Theatre:

Actors:

BRIAN . . . . Orion Bradshaw

SARAH . . . . Sophie Green

FRED . . . . Adrian de Forest

FRANK . . . . Scott Fullerton

GRETA . . . . Luci Bedel

GERTRUDE . . . . Kristin Martz

Director: G. Valmont Thomas

Date of Production: Ashland 10-minute play festival, 2005

NORTH POLE WINTER WOES

Theatre: Toyboat Productions

Actors:

SANTA . . . . Jarrett Brown

ELF . . . . Aaron Ross

SAM . . . . Isaac Koval

Director: David C. Rosenbaum

Date of Production: December, 2006

DEATH AND JAVIER MIGUEL GUADELAJARA ASANTE

Theatre: Northwest Playwright's Guild

Actors:

DEATH . . . . Frank Faro

JOSÉ . . . . Alex Rodriguez

SAMUEL . . . . Bud Reece

Director: Susan Chamberlain

Date of Production: April-Foolery Short Play Showcase, 2000

TONGUE, TIED

A SHORT PLAY

CHARACTERS

TINA. A young woman with different colored socks on each hand. Her socks are **JEAN-CLAUDE** *(left hand) and* **LATISHA** *(right hand).*

TOM. A young man with different colored socks on each hand. His socks are **MR. CHAN** *(left hand) and* **SVEN** *(right hand).*

(A psychiatrist's waiting room. **TINA** *sits, hands hidden behind her, waiting. After a moment her right hand jumps.)*

TINA. Stop it.

(Again her right hand jumps.)

I said, STOP IT.

(Again her right hand jumps.)

Latisha! Damn it! I said, STOP!

*(***TINA** *begins struggling to keep her right hand behind her.)*

No…no….I said….NO. No-no-no-no no-no. Latisha…!

*(***TINA***'s right hand –* **LATISHA** *– bolts out and looks around.)*

LATISHA. Girl, how many times have I told you? You gotta stop keepin' us down like that. Look at this bright, crazy world you're trying to keep us from. Just look at it! Ain't it amazin'?!

TINA. Latisha, you know I'm not trying to keep you down. I'm attempting to live an ordinary and relatively content life.

LATISHA. Ain't we all, sista. Ain't we all.

TINA. And having a black woman, who happens….

LATISHA. A proud, powerful woman of color. Thank you.

TINA. Exactly. A proud, powerful woman of color, who happens to be a sock, living on my hand….

LATISHA. Hey, you can't just blame me. I thought there was also some hot, little piece of French crème brulée dancin' on your other mitten?

(A slight pause as **TINA** *fights with her left hand.)*

Ain't that right?

(More struggling and then **TINA***'s left hand –* **JEAN-CLAUDE** *– bursts forth.)*

JEAN-CLAUDE. Bien sur! Parceque we will revolt and lop your pretty bourgeois head off!

LATISHA. Jean-Claude, why do you always opt for over-dramatic reactionism, when intelligent discourse can....

JEAN-CLAUDE. Latisha, you and your intelligent discourse can suck my left....

TINA. People, people, people...please! Can we not simply sit here and get along? Isn't that what I've been attempting? To coordinate vast and diametrically opposed perspectives since I acquired you two.

JEAN-CLAUDE. Acquired? More like forced encampment.

LATISHA. Yeah, acquired, my big, beautiful ass. If I remember right, some dude named Matt dumped your skinny rump and you were all...

JEAN-CLAUDE. ...Oh, boo-hoo. Oh, boo-hoo. Look at me I'm all alone.

LATISHA. No one loves me. I wish I weren't soooo forlorn. Soooo despondent, dejected and alone.

TINA. I didn't say....

JEAN-CLAUDE. Mon cher, I'm afraid you did. And voila, we is ici.

LATISHA. That's right. We're here and there's no way you can blame us.

TINA. Yes, well....It might be different if you two didn't bicker and argue so much. I might be able to enjoy your company. However...

*(***TOM*** enters. His hands are thrust deep in his jacket pockets. ***TINA*** hides her hands behind her. ***TOM*** sits. A long, long uncomfortable silence. A few twitches from both their respective backs and pockets.)*

TINA. Can you believe how hot it is?

TOM. I know. Why just the other day I could swear I saw a dog burst into flames. A dog didn't actually catch fire....

TINA. It seems like it's a million degrees out there. I don't really mean a million degrees....

TINA/TOM. That'd be crazy.

(TINA *and* TOM *struggle to keep their hands hidden. However, to no avail. Simultaneously* LATISHA, JEAN-CLAUDE, MR. CHAN, *and* SVEN *leap out.*)

SVEN. Tom, if I'm not mistaken, keeping any part of your consciousness purposefully in the dark, regardless how unwanted, is perhaps not the best coping mechanism.

MR. CHAN. I've no idea what he just said, but I will agree with it.

JEAN-CLAUDE. Mademoiselle, what'd I say about your bourgeois head?

LATISHA. Girl, are you not thinkin'? Keep this up I'll help the little Frenchie.

JEAN-CLAUDE. Little? Moi? I'll have you know my nickname is Mont Blanc.

SVEN. Mont Blanc?

LATISHA. And who is this cutie? Hello.

(TINA *and* TOM *shove their hands away.*)

TOM. My father was a magician in the Tibetan army during the occupation of New Zealand in 1972.

TINA. I'm an entertainer. My show is in Vegas.

TOM. Every night he would entertain the troops with magic and vaudeville.

TINA. I inherited my act from a crazy, one-legged aunt who raised me after my parents were devoured by bunnies on a Tuesday during a solar eclipse.

TOM. Then during the month the natives call Rama-rama a witch doctor cast a spell on his socks.

TINA. My one-legged aunt was very strict and hated fingerprints on anything, thus I became conditioned to wear socks on my hands.

TOM. The next morning Sven and Mr. Chan had arrived–invariably I have inherited the curse.

TINA/TOM. Honestly, I'm not crazy.

(Beat. Gradually **LATISHA**, **JEAN-CLAUDE**, **SVEN**, *and* **MR. CHAN** *slip out of the shadows.)*

TINA. I'm…I'm Tina.

TOM. Hello. I'm Tom.

JEAN-CLAUDE. And I'm a turtle dove.

MR. CHAN. Tom, if you want, I'll kick his ass. Now.

SVEN. Violence is the first choice of the ignorant.

MR. CHAN. And after French frying Frenchie, I'll teach Sven about the philosophy of the fist.

JEAN-CLAUDE. From a hospital bed. Prepare to be Jean-Clobbered.

LATISHA. Is that Tom with one M, or two?

TOM. Just…just one.

LATISHA. Ain't goin' ta do. Don't you know the ladies like things double sized?

TINA. Latisha! I thought we agreed you wouldn't….

TOM. Well, I…I guess I'm willing to add a letter….

JEAN-CLAUDE. Ah, what a pansy, he'll change anything – even his name – at the drop of a hat.

TOM. No, but for the right woman I'm willing to….

JEAN-CLAUDE. Boo! Now you can change your panties, too. Hahahahahaha!

MR. CHAN. Let me kick his ass. Let me beat that French smirk off his….

TOM. Mr. Chan, no. No. Remember the song? The song Mr. Chan…the song…War?

MR. CHAN. War? What's it good for?

TOM. Absolutely nothing.

JEAN-CLAUDE. Singing, little pansy, I would make pâté out of you.

SVEN. Ignore him, Mr. Chan. His anger and frustration is from not having found love.

LATISHA. I knew there was a reason I liked you. War?! What's it good for?

MR. CHAN. Absolutely nothing!

LATISHA. Say it again!

MR. CHAN. Absolutely nothing!

LATISHA. Mr. Chan you rock. Come here, honey!

MR. CHAN. This bee is bringing the honey, baby! Bzzzzzz....

(**LATISHA** *and* **MR. CHAN** *begin kissing.*)

TINA. She's always like this.

TOM. Yeah, Mr. Chan has a tendency towards the ladies.

(*Suddenly,* **JEAN-CLAUDE** *and* **SVEN**, *lunge at one another. They, too, begin kissing.*)

TINA. It…it must be the heat.

TOM. Uh, yeah…yeah…the…the heat. *(beat)* So…so, what brings you here to Doctor DeMarco's?

TINA. Um. The…uh…honestly? Latisha and Jean-Claude. What about you?

TOM. Me too. Mr. Chan and Sven.

(*Beat as* **TINA** *and* **TOM** *watch the puppets necking.*)

TINA. Love 'em, but….*(beat)* Your…your father wasn't a magician with the Tibetan army, was he?

TOM. No. And you don't have a crazy, one-legged aunt?

TINA. No.

TOM. And your parents probably weren't eaten by bunnies during a solar eclipse? *(beat)* You know, I just want to be normal. I want to be able to get a coffee and not worry if Sven is going to complain about holding the scalding cup, let alone his snide comments about the caffeine, the sugar, and the creamer.

(**SVEN** *breaks from* **JEAN-CLAUDE**.)

SVEN. It's a vasoconstrictor. Don't blame me if you have a massive coronary some lonely night while watching *Desperate Housewives.*

(**SVEN** *and* **JEAN-CLAUDE** *resume kissing.*)

TINA. Yes, normal would be nice. Like picking flowers without Jean-Claude calling me une pansy de la fleur du mal. Or Latisha complaining about her allergies.

TOM. Hey, pollen is nothing to laugh...about. I've...I've allergies, too.

TINA. Confession: I bloat up like a balloon if I even see shellfish.

TOM. Mr. Chan too – regular Goodyear blimp.

TINA. Jean-Claude's afraid of heights. You should hear him wail like a baby when I pick apples.

(JEAN-CLAUDE breaks from SVEN. MR. CHAN and LATISHA stop kissing to listen.)

JEAN-CLAUDE. I do not wail – I weep. I weep from the realization that life is fleeting, and your picking an apple is the perfect representation of a life lived and lost. Regardless how perfect the fruit, Death shall eat it to the core and, ultimately, cast it aside for the ants and worms to finish. Life is a mime at a convention for the blind.

(Beat. All ponder. MR. CHAN and LATISHA, JEAN-CLAUDE and SVEN lunge back together, kissing more desperately. Beat.)

TOM. It's gotta be the heat.

TINA. Do you think we should try and stop them?

TOM. This is the most time I've had to myself in months. Not...not to imply that you're not great company, but....

TINA. No, no. I know exactly what you mean. *(beat)*

TOM. It's weird, isn't it?

TINA. Incredibly. *(beat)* There's got to be a way to get rid of them, don't you think?

TOM. Have you tried doing giant loads of laundry?

TINA. My record is ten in one day – lost two pairs of jeans, three blouses, a sweatshirt, and a skirt I didn't even wash.

TOM. My golden retriever, Mr. Snickers, will chew a lead pipe before them. They blow out the matches, and refuse to go near moving machinery parts. They curl into the fetal position any time I get near scissors, or knives. I've even attempted to talk to a surgeon….

TINA. About…amputation?

(Beat as **LATISHA, MR. CHAN, SVEN,** *and* **JEAN-CLAUDE** *hover threateningly.)*

TOM. Yes.

TINA. Uh…uh, can you believe how hot it is?

TOM. I've always hated hot weather.

TINA. Me too. The humid, stillness causes the sweat to collect at the nape of your neck and behind your knees.

TOM. And forces your underwear to crawl up your crack….

*(***LATISHA** *and* **MR. CHAN, SVEN** *and* **JEAN-CLAUDE** *return to necking.)*

TINA. And you can't sleep at night with the windows open….

TOM. Because the creepy man in the bushes is going to….

TINA. Crawl through the window.

TOM. Exactly.

TOM/TINA. It drives me crazy.

(beat)

TOM. Crazy.

TINA. Crazy.

TOM. You're crazy.

TINA. I'm not crazy. You're crazy.

TOM. Nooo.

(beat)

TOM/TINA. We're crazy.

*(***LATISHA** *and* **MR. CHAN** *separate, post coital.)*

MR. CHAN. Man without horse doesn't buy saddle.

LATISHA. Yeah, you don't kill the rooster if the hen's happy.

TOM. Well...Sven, when he's brooding over the chessboard with a glass of Akvavit does claim....

(SVEN disengages from JEAN-CLAUDE.)

SVEN. If time and space are relative, it would seem prudent to assume "reality" is also relative. Therefore, one could postulate each individual has their own inherent reality, thus providing the possibility to surmise those without talking socks on their hands are the minority. And, in regards to genetics, anomalies often....

JEAN-CLAUDE. Often fuse opposing poles together, like amore. N'est pas?

TOM. Of course, there's the conundrum...what happens to us when they're gone?

TINA. We return to...to....

JEAN-CLAUDE. Weeping.

SVEN. Brooding.

TOM. You...you weep?

TINA. Life is a mime at a convention for the blind. *(beat)* And you? You brood?

TOM. Time. Space. Relativity. Sweet, sad, silent...consuming...oblivion.

TINA. I-crochet. I-disdain-green-M & M's. I-prefer-tea-to-coffee. I-fear....

LATISHA. Girl, will you shut up and kiss the One-M fool!

MR. CHAN. Yeah, Tom, thump her with those thin lips.

LATISHA. Kiss him!

(beat)

JEAN-CLAUDE. Weep not and...slip your hand...slowly... here.

SVEN. Glide past the dark despair...and...settle...here.

(beat)

TINA. But...but we could be doomed. Doomed to... lonely, ice cream nights of *Desperate Housewives*.

TOM. We…we could.

JEAN-CLAUDE. Oui?

TOM. We – you and I. Not oui.

TINA. Right. You and I. Not oui. *(beat)*

MR. CHAN. We.

LATISHA. We. *(beat)*

TINA. We.

SVEN. Oui.

LATISHA. We.

MR. CHAN. Oui.

SVEN. Wee-wee.

TOM. Oui.

TOM/TINA. We….

> *(beat)*

TOM. I mean, they seem to have done pretty well. Right?

> (**LATISHA**, **MR. CHAN**, **SVEN** *and* **JEAN-CLAUDE** *nod in agreement.*)

> Why can't we?

TINA. All we…us can do is…is try.

TOM. Oui?

TINA. Yes. Oui. Us and…every….

TOM/TINA. One….

> (**TINA** *and* **TOM** *tentatively kiss. Gradually they continue with enthusiasm.* **LATISHA**, **MR. CHAN**, **JEAN-CLAUDE** *and* **SVEN** *watch, turn to the audience, take a bow and resume kissing as the lights fade.*)

End

DEATH AND JAVIER MIGUEL LOPEZ GUADALAJARA ASANTE

A SHORT PLAY

CHARACTERS

JOSÉ. A young barista.
DEATH. The stark and somber collector of souls.
SAMUEL. A city worker with a penchant for philosophy.

*(The stage is dark. **DEATH**'s voice is heard asking the time. As he enters and moves about the lights slowly come up. Eventually morning is represented and **DEATH** finds **JOSÉ** rolling his portable espresso cart to a downtown street corner where he begins setting up.)*

DEATH. Pardon me? Mrs. Denise Evans? Do you know the time? Midnight? Yes, thank you. Excuse me, David Smith, what time is it? 3:15? Thanks very much. Sue Geller? What time is it? 4:20? Great. Thanks. Ah, Dr. Marcus Jenkins? Do you have the time? 5:45? Wonderful, thank you very much. Ah, my good barista, Javier, do you know what time it is?

JOSÉ. Yes, I do. It's mornin' time – which means coffee, man. Time for a mega-latte, or an atomic-mocha. Though with your complexion, and it's a wonderful and healthy pale one, don't get me wrong, I'm just saying to pop some color onto those pallid cheeks I might indulge, go whole hog, shoot the works, jump the train, bury the hatchet, kick the dog, throw the cat, and get the concentrated tornado of caffeine – The Mind Wedgie. That's right The Mind Wedgie – guaranteed to pull your shorts through your skull. What do you say? What do you say? Huh? $2.35. Best deal in downtown. What do you say? Yes? No? What do you say? What do you say?

DEATH. You are Javier Miguel Lopez Guadalajara Asante, are you not?

*(**SAMUEL** enters with a broom and a trash can on wheels in search of things to pick up.)*

JOSÉ. Man, The Wedgie is what you need. Picture this – I grind six, six man, six chocolate covered coffee beans, add four shots of espresso, fill with whole milk, two shakes of cinnamon, a dash of nutmeg, a quick squirt of whipped cream and you are wedgin' in style. Skyrocket in flight, baby. Everyone's getin' 'em. Everyone.

DEATH. Are you Javier Miguel Lopez Guadalajara Asante?

JOSÉ. Hey, Samuel! Samuel, doesn't everyone get The Mind Wedgie? The Wedgie is where it's at, right? Right, man? Samuel! Hey!

DEATH. I don't believe it's necessary to disturb the poor gentleman. If you'd just simply answer my question.

JOSÉ. Samuel, over here. Hey, man, how's it goin'? Great. Great. Look, tell the man about how The Wedgie is the best thing around.

SAMUEL. I wouldn't say "great." Not with the precarious state of the world. More like an aroused melancholy, if you will.

JOSÉ. No, no philosophy Sam. Tell him about The Wedgie. The Wedgie, man.

SAMUEL. I don't consider myself a philosopher. Philosophers tend to be corrupted by their predilection for the vices of academia. Socratic doctrine and the such tends to taint what's actually happening on the street, in the world, thus diminishing....

JOSÉ. Sam. Hey, Samuel. Easy big boy, just about The Wedgie. Okay? He's had a couple dozen too many.

DEATH. Yes, well if you'd just answer....

JOSÉ. Samuel? The Wedgie – it's tasty, isn't it? It's good, yeah?

SAMUEL. Yes. In a pungent and dramatic coffee sense of tasty, yes. However, good would imply that coffee has the capacity for moral judgment. Which, unless I'm mistaken, it hasn't actually achieved cognition. Though there are certain plants in the Brazilian rain forest that have demonstrated some remarkable attributes akin to consciousness.

JOSÉ. Thanks Sam. Thank you, Samuel. Samuel.... Here, take this, for your troubles. You may return to your beloved streets. So, what do you say? Mind Wedgie for ya?

DEATH. I have come for you Javier Miguel Lopez Guadalajara Asante – I am the great Specter, I am Death. Come.

JOSÉ. Whoa! You've had enough, man. A Wedgie would put you in a coma. Man, you gotta tell me these things– I could be liable if you have a heart attack or something. Single, de-caf, almond latte for you, bud. Speculator in Death, huh? Much money in that? What do you deal in cemetery commodities? Tombstones, rosaries, candles and that liquid stuff they keep dead frogs in. What's it called? Smells real bad and....

DEATH. Formaldehyde.

JOSÉ. Yeah, that's it. You know they got people drinking that now? Call themselves the walking dead.

DEATH. Mere acquaintances. Now, are you Javier Miguel Lopez Guadalajara Asante, or not?

JOSÉ. No, I am not. Besides what the hell you want José for?

DEATH. I want Javier Miguel Lopez Guadalajara Asante, not José.

JOSÉ. Then you don't know Javier Miguel Lopez Guadalajara Asante– because everyone, everyone that's his friend, calls him José.

DEATH. Then are you José?

JOSÉ. No, man, I'm Manuel.

DEATH. When do you expect Javier Miguel...forgive me. When do you expect José to be here?

JOSÉ. Why?

DEATH. I've an appointment with Javier Miguel – José. You see, as I have said, I'm Death, and I'm a little pressed for time.

JOSÉ. Aren't we all. Aren't we all.

DEATH. Some have less than others. But, as I was saying.... It was my understanding Javier Miguel – José – would be here. We would conduct a quick and efficient transaction and I would be on my way.

JOSÉ. Oh, man, he owes you money too? How much? Shit, after that Oregon game he probably owes everyone in town.

DEATH. No, that was simply a colloquial use of words. What....

JOSÉ. No wonder he wanted the day off – the rat bastard.

DEATH. What I meant to say was I would rip his soul out through his ear and shove him through Hell's keyhole. You see... I'm Death. My card.

(Hands **JOSÉ** *business card.)*

JOSÉ. You know I don't think you should have any syrup. Let's just say a skinny de-caf. And besides you get José after I'm done with him.

DEATH. I don't believe you understand the situation Manuel. You see....

JOSÉ. Oh, I understand it. I understand Manuel's getin' screwed again. I get my ass out in this frigid morning to do José a favor – I even let him borrow my car to go to Seattle with his chica, and...AND my first customer is Death. Who, by the way, owes me a buck ninety-five. Is that about right? Do I have that correct, Death?

DEATH. Actually, yes, it would seem so. However....

JOSÉ. No, no, no. No, howevers, buts, maybes, or ors. That's just the way it is, okay? And what exactly do you expect me to do? Pull José out of my ass?

DEATH. If I thought it possible – yes.

JOSÉ. Oh, check it out Sam, Death's pulling attitude. I'm tryin' to make some bank here, so I can send it to my parents in the old country and you're givin' me attitude, well, fuck you. I got better things to do in the morning than talk to assholes like you.

*(***JOSÉ*** *pushes cart away from one corner to another.)*

DEATH. Yes, but...I say...You see...It's like this....

(There is the sound of a cellular phone ringing.)

Oh, no, it's the boss.

JOSÉ. The boss?

DEATH. Ignorant mortal – The Devil, Lucifer, Satan, Beelzebub, et cetera, et cetera.

(DEATH *pulls cell phone out from jacket. Clears throat and answers.*)

Plague riddled morning, Death here, grimmest of the grim reapers, how may I help you? Oh, it's you sir. Well, uh, yes sir. But…No. No. It's just that…Yes, sir. The name's Javier Miguel Lopez Guadalajara Asante–José to his friends. Well, I'm sorry, sir, but that's what was on my invoice this morning. After him? Let's see… another couple of hundred. Sorry. Exactly, precisely, 8,559. Yes, sir. But. Very well. Good…bye.

(DEATH *hangs up and ponders for a moment.*)

Listen, Manuel, I'll be honest with you, okay? You don't mind do you? It's been so long since I've had a heart to heart with anyone. I mean anytime I get close to someone they die on me. It's just hard, you know? Always alone, wandering spectral ether. It's just not as fun as it was. Now it's just numbers. Doesn't matter who, when, where, just how many today Death? Is that all Death? You missed Jones in Duluth, Yoshida in Nagasaki, and Andronisi in Athens. Anymore it's just numbers and quotas. You ever try and come up with a new plague? It was easy in the good old days, before microbiologists and immunologists, and bastards like that. Just needed a few rats, a few colonists – hell it was easy then. But now you've got to take your time. Figure out branched amino acid chains and DNA catalysts and…. And then we've got less demons in the field – it's getting over crowded in hell, so we're having to place more emphasis on administration – which means more work for me. It's just not fair.

JOSÉ. What about automation? Computers? Work from home? Cyborg-daemons, or something?

DEATH. No, the old man still likes the hands on approach.

JOSÉ. Yeah, everybody appreciates the personal touch.

DEATH. Just shows ya care.

JOSÉ. Oh, yeah.

DEATH. He likes to say there's nothing like looking a client in the eye and wrenching their soul into the fiery pits. I'll admit I've grown to like that part.

JOSÉ. Didn't at first?

DEATH. God no. Before Satan picked up my contract I was a free agent for a few millennia. That's when I had it cush. Subcontracting to both sides. Upstairs – Downstairs. Both were just getting off the ground. Attempting to get a market presence. Promising this, promising that. And there I was sit'n pretty in the middle. Everybody's golden boy. Then Satan made an offer I couldn't refuse. Damn typical.

JOSÉ. You sold out?

DEATH. Yeah. Shorter commute, a handful of little perks – attend assassinations, have a major plague named after me, battle side seats for wars – but, all in all, the work became just so…so…

JOSÉ. Mundane? Trivial? Passé? Boring? Monotonous?

DEATH. Yes, monotonous. Everyone I met was going to hell. It lacked variety. And then over time I lost my edge. Just didn't care. And then it got so damn crowded. Productivity went up, but the quality just plummeted. Before the rush you could sit and lounge for a while. Discuss their lives with them, give them a little closure, a little perspective. Not any more. Shove 'em in, hand 'em a pamphlet, and off ya go for another sad soul.

JOSÉ. Sounds tough.

DEATH. It affects you, you know? Affects your sanity, your practicality for choosing fruit, for defensive driving, for remembering song lyrics, for attempting to make sense of it all.

JOSÉ. Hey, hey, sit here. Sit. Relax. Take a load off. Here have a mega-vita-juice.

DEATH. No, no, really I can't.

JOSÉ. Don't worry, it's on the house.

DEATH. No, I've got a quota to reach. Souls to escort. I need to find Javier Miguel Lopez Guadalajara Asante.

JOSÉ. José.

DEATH. Yes, I need to find José. And then there's....

JOSÉ. Listen to me. Listen! You're pale as a ghost and thin as a skeleton, and even for you it's probably not too healthy. What you need is some down time, some you time, some vitamins and relaxation. Now drink the mega-vita-juice and relax. Drink it. I'm going to go talk to Samuel, maybe we can come up with something.

DEATH. No, I don't think....

JOSÉ. God, no wonder you're on Satan's black list, you don't listen, or follow instructions very well. Now just shut up and sit there. (**JOSÉ** *gets up and walks to* **SAMUEL.**) Christ, Death is a pain in the ass. Hey, Sam, got a little problem, can I talk to you?

SAMUEL. Of course. Though to classify a problem as 'little' implies certain relative proportions, all things being relative your 'little' could be someone's 'large'. That's to say....

JOSÉ. Yeah, okay. Whatever. Listen.

(**JOSÉ** *pulls* **SAMUEL** *over and quickly, silently briefs him. For a few moments they discuss things with much shaking and nodding of heads. Finally they agree, shake hands, part, and walk to where* **DEATH** *has made himself comfortable.*)

Hey, Death, I think we got somethin' for ya.

DEATH. This is very good. You know, I do feel better.

JOSÉ. Well; it's got plenty of vitamins, minerals, bee pollen, echinacea, and stuff. But listen....

DEATH. Don't suppose I could get this delivered, do you? Maybe a case, or two, every so often?

JOSÉ. Delivered? To hell?

DEATH. No. No. I live in a suburb. Hell has gone to hell, so to speak. Crime. Pollution. Urban sprawl. Everything. And I don't care what the old man says it's out of hand.

JOSÉ. A suburb?

DEATH. Well, actually old town, Hades. It's a little three bedroom pumice bungalow. A few minutes by ferry to Hell proper, where the furnaces and pits are. On a clear day you can almost see the fires.

JOSÉ. Nice, sounds very nice.

DEATH. Perhaps someday you can visit.

JOSÉ. Uh, yeah, maybe. But listen, about José, about your predicament....

SAMUEL. I think you should go.

JOSÉ. What?

SAMUEL. Forget about death quitting....

DEATH. Excuse me?

SAMUEL. ...I think you should visit hell. Imagine the insight and understanding you'd return with? You might be another savior. Someone to....

DEATH. Yes, there's much to learn there, but you want me to quit?

SAMUEL. Not really quit, more like....

JOSÉ. Yeah. Quit. Retire. Finis. No mas.

DEATH. But...but...I couldn't do that. I'm not that close to retirement. I'd need a job. And what about health insurance? A place to stay? I'm sure to be evicted. Yes, I hate my job, but the company provides everything. What would I do?

JOSÉ. Write a memoir.

SAMUEL. Instant best seller.

JOSÉ. Do talk shows.

SAMUEL. Instant celebrity.

DEATH. But I'm an integral part of nature, of the natural law. Without me, if you'll excuse the pun, all hell would break loose. You can't even cope with the populace now, what happens when....

SAMUEL. Actually you're slowly being fazed out – modern medicine, robotics, science – eventually death will be obsolete and will be more a personal choice than a natural imperative.

DEATH. That's blasphemy! Take that back. You take that back or so help me I'll kill you where you stand.

JOSÉ. Easy Death. Easy. Weren't you the one who mentioned the geneticists and all…all that?

DEATH. Yes. Yes, I was.

JOSÉ. And how it just wasn't the same? Look at you, just look at you. Pale, distraught, threatening mere philosophers.

SAMUEL. I'd take offense, but philosophically I understand your position, so silent I remain.

JOSÉ. Besides Samuel here has done some writing himself. He could help you. He's got some great ideas for titles, and….

DEATH. Well, what about the souls I still need to escort? I can't very well….

JOSÉ. Listen Death, you leave that to me. Just worry about yourself. Get a cabin in the woods, a golden retriever to sit at your feet, a case of good scotch, a typewriter and just relax and write. I can wing the whole escorting lost souls to hell thing. Don't you worry. I'm serious, I can take care of it.

DEATH. I'll do it! Damn if you're not right. I do deserve to be happy!

(**DEATH** *takes phone out and dials.*)

Yes, hello? Would you please relay to the boss that I quit. Thank you. Here. And take this. And this too.

(*Hands* **JOSÉ** *phone, day planner, and keys.*)

Thanks, Manuel, I'll dedicate the book to you.

JOSÉ. Well, thanks, but that's not necessary. Just….

DEATH. Now Sam, what were those titles?

SAMUEL. First there's Death Discusses Life.

DEATH. Oh, I like that. I like that.

SAMUEL. Another – Death On Life.

DEATH. Oh, yes, I like that too. All these choices. This is going to be difficult.

SAMUEL. Fortunately, or unfortunately, that's all life is – choices.

DEATH. What about an agent and a publisher? Do you think I need a pseudonym? Death, it's just so, so one dimensional. Perhaps something with a little more pizzazz?

(DEATH and SAMUEL exit. Phone begins to ring and ring and ring. Finally JOSÉ answers.)

JOSÉ. Uh, hello?

(The stage resounds with SATAN's deep, catastrophic voice.)

SATAN. WHO IS THIS?

JOSÉ. Uh, um, my...my friends call me José.

(Lights out.)

End

(")CLOWN(S)(")(?)

A SHORT PLAY

CHARACTERS

DWAYNE. Dude The Kid Clown.
JARVIS. Dwayne's Flute Playing Side-kick.
CARRIE EVERLY. Single Mother.
SERGEANT BURK. Police Officer.
PRIVATE HANS. Burk's Side-kick.

*(It's a late afternoon in a small, unassuming city park. Atop a jungle gym sits **DWAYNE**, a kid's party clown, attempting to make a balloon animal. Occasionally he drinks from a bottle wrapped in a paper bag. There is a pile of rubber balloon discards beneath him. Nearby, under a tree, sits **JARVIS**, barefoot, twittering on a flute. **JARVIS** can only speak in "Flutese," i.e. via a bright red, plastic flute.)*

DWAYNE. Damn that kid. Damn him to hell.

*(**DWAYNE** throws latest balloon animal attempt to the ground, drinks, and starts over. **JARVIS** comments.)*

No one asked you, Jarvis, so shut up.

*(**JARVIS** plays sarcastic.)*

Shut up!

*(**JARVIS** challenges.)*

I said…. Fine.

*(**DWAYNE** quickly makes a balloon dog, a pig and a horse.)*

Dog. Pig. Horse. Satisfied?

*(**JARVIS** whistles his agreement.)*

Wonderful – the parade can commence.

*(Beat as **DWAYNE** continues attempting to make another animal. After a moment **JARVIS** plays a woeful comment.)*

I know. I know. It was the cornerstone to my menagerie. My whole tumble act flowed from it. Then the jokes, and finally a little magic, and bam I'm done and gone. But…but without it…without this one stupid, friggin' animal I've got nothing. Nothing.

*(**JARVIS** plays.)*

Hey, that kid was out of line. So…so out of line. He might as well have been on a Tasmanian yacht fishing for Narwhales.

(**JARVIS** *comments.*)

Whatever. You know what I mean. I…I mean I…I didn't know what to do. Besides, the kid deserved it. If he hadn't of popped off and….

(**JARVIS** *comments.*)

I know. I know. I just stood there dumbfounded that I couldn't make it. Years and years, thousands of Kid Stacy and Kid David parties, and I…I can't make my animal. I mean, I'm famous for that frigging animal. People sign me up based on just that.

(**JARVIS** *plays.*)

I've had nightmares about these stupid animals tearing me limb from limb, but never did I think I couldn't make one. Never. It was an impossibility.

(**JARVIS** *comments.*)

Obviously it's possible. It happened, didn't it?

(**JARVIS** *plays.*)

Shut up.

(**PRIVATE HANS** *enters. He looks* **DWAYNE** *and* **JARVIS** *over.* **DWAYNE** *drinks as* **JARVIS** *gives a brief explanation.*)

Beat it Billy Boo-Hoo before the wind blows you back into yesterday.

(**PRIVATE HANS** *exits quickly.* **JARVIS** *comments.*)

Will you quit pointing out the obvious?

(**JARVIS** *plays.*)

No, he's just a security punk. Not some city cop. Right?

(**JARVIS** *plays. Beat as* **DWAYNE** *makes another attempt.*)

Shit. It's over, under, over, twist, twist...shit. Goddamn it. I...I can't get it.

(**JARVIS** *plays.*)

Hey, you take that back. You take that back right now, right here, or I kick your ass.

(**JARVIS** *plays.*)

How many times do I have to tell you love's got nothing to do with it? Okay?

(**JARVIS** *plays.*)

Yeah, she was attractive, but so what? Dime a dozen, right?

(**JARVIS** *comments.*)

Look, I was there to do a job, and I wasn't going to let some attractive skirt get in the way. You may not get this, but there's such a thing as honor and duty among clowns. And I, for one, believe in it, and attempt at all times to uphold it.

(**JARVIS** *comments.*)

You want me to come down there and kick your ass? Because I will. I told you before it wasn't because of her.

(**JARVIS** *plays a long, slow, plaintive piece.* **DWAYNE** *nods in sad agreement.*)

You're right. Absolutely. Absolutely. Yes, I'll admit, I've seduced a mom, or two, in my day. But, honestly, what clown hasn't?

(**JARVIS** *plays.*)

Jarvis, you know Bongo Bob's gay.

(**JARVIS** *plays.*)

That's it – I'm going to kick your ass.

(**DWAYNE** *jumps down and twists his ankle.*)

Ouch, goddamn it.

*(**JARVIS** plays.)*

Shut up! It's not karma. And, it's not about love.

*(**JARVIS** plays.)*

That's it.

*(**DWAYNE** quickly limps over and attempts to assault **JARVIS**. **JARVIS** shoves **DWAYNE** back. **DWAYNE** trips and falls under jungle gym. Beat. **JARVIS** plays something apologetic.)*

I don't care.

*(**JARVIS** plays. **CARRIE** enters unnoticed by **DWAYNE**.)*

No! I am not in love with her.

*(**JARVIS** plays a question.)*

I said I did not fall in love with her. I never met her before. How could I possibly fall in love with her? Clowns don't fall in love at first sight. Okay? Not at her first words – Hi, you must be Dude the Kid Clown. Not at the subtle scent of her vanilla laced perfume. Not at the bright, green-gold glint of her eyes. Not, and I emphasize, NOT at first sight. Okay? It takes time to fall in love. You discover her likes and dislikes. Little quirks of personality. Dreams and aspirations. Maybe those coincide with yours and you think, yeah, yeah, this could work. Then – and only then – after months of compiling information, comparing and contrasting mutual experiences, does a clown fall in love. Only then, Jarvis. Only then. Not, and I repeat, not at first sight. Shit, where's my bourbon?

CARRIE. I believe it's up there, Mr. Dude.

DWAYNE. Jarvis, that's her, isn't it?

*(**JARVIS** plays.)*

Perfect. Why didn't you tell me?

*(**JARVIS** plays.)*

Jarvis, I am, one day, going to kick your ass from here to Hoboken and back, and I swear....

CARRIE. Uh, Mr. Dude?

DWAYNE. I will get you for this, Jarvis. If it's the last thing I do. I swear….

CARRIE. Excuse me, Mr. Dude?

DWAYNE. Please, Ms. Everly, call me Dwayne.

CARRIE. Dwayne?

DWAYNE. Yes, Ms. Everly?

CARRIE. Call me Carrie.

DWAYNE. Gladly. Now, Ms. Carrie, what brings you to this small, unassuming city park? Is it, perhaps, the existential implications of my skeleton joke?

CARRIE. Sorry?

(**JARVIS** *plays something forgiving.*)

DWAYNE. Jarvis, stay out of this. Carrie, it's my skeleton joke – Why didn't the skeleton cross the road?

CARRIE. I'm sorry, Dwayne, but…..

DWAYNE. Because it didn't have the guts. It's very controversial among the West Hill mothers. I've been banned in Aloha and Beaverton because of it.

(**JARVIS** *plays something.*)

I am too. Now shut up.

CARRIE. Uh, Dwayne, I'm here because I need to pay you. Your roommate said you might be here.

DWAYNE. You owe me nothing.

CARRIE. I do. I believe two hundred dollars for….

DWAYNE. No. I was unable to perform. My fingers fumbled with the limp casing of what should've been a majestic animal. After that failure it was an absolutely hollow and unemotional performance. You owe me nothing.

(**JARVIS** *plays.*)

Shut up.

CARRIE. Well, I suppose if he does owe you and doesn't want it….

DWAYNE. Look, I don't need you paying my debts, okay?

Clowns, such as I, do have a certain amount of pride and dignity in upholding their responsibilities – both financial and social – without interference from meddling mothers.

CARRIE. Then take the money.

DWAYNE. I don't want it.

(**JARVIS** *plays.*)

Jarvis, shut up.

CARRIE. Then what do you want?

DWAYNE. What do I want?

CARRIE. Yes. What….

DWAYNE. What, possibly, could a kid's clown want?

(**JARVIS** *plays sarcastic.* **CARRIE** *laughs.*)

No, that's not it. Do you really want to know what I want? I want to work for an ad agency writing bright, shiny buzz lyrics for pathetic products that people sing about in the shower. I want to wear thin Italian shoes and drink young, tannic French Bordeaux. I want to drive a domestic SUV that destroys the ozone even when it's parked. I want an overpriced, luxury closet-condo in the most crowded part of the city. I want a private chef who cooks all day, so I can throw it away at night, while the homeless starve outside. But, mostly…I want to go out with you. I want to find out if you like sushi and sleeping in on Sundays, or crosswords and Jackie Chan movies. I want to discover every annoying little habit of yours that'll make me crazy. And, in the middle of the night, when you get that intolerably squeaky nose whistle and I lie awake staring at the ceiling, I want to know that even then, in the very pit of insomniatic hell, I love you. That…that is what I want. I want to love you. I want to be cast out to sea without hope of salvation knowing the only thing of consequence keeping me afloat and from the dark, cold depths is my love for you. That's what I want. Okay?

CARRIE. Wow. Yeah. Okay.

(**JARVIS** *plays in agreement.*)

DWAYNE. So…that's what I want.

CARRIE. Dwayne, that's probably the sweetest….

    (**SERGEANT BURK** *and* **PRIVATE HANS** *enter.*)

SGT. BURK. You there, clown, we've got a couple of questions for you.

    (**JARVIS** *plays.*)

You stay out of this flute player.

    (**JARVIS** *plays.*)

PRVT. HANS. Watch him, Burk. He looks like trouble to me.

    (**JARVIS** *plays.*)

SGT. BURK. Right. You cover Zamphyr. I've got the clown. Now, clown, I want you to put the balloons down and step away from the jungle gym very, very slowly. No false moves. Got it?

CARRIE. Officer, what's he done?

SGT. BURK. Ma'am, this doesn't concern you. So, if you'd please, step back.

DWAYNE. Look, Officer, you've got the wrong clown. I haven't done anything.

    (**JARVIS** *plays.*)

Jarvis, shut up.

CARRIE. I thought Joey Fredericks hit little Timmy?

    (**JARVIS** *plays.*)

DWAYNE. Jarvis!

CARRIE. And my underwear drawer?

    (**JARVIS** *plays.*)

DWAYNE. Jarvis, shut up, or I'm going to kick your ass. I've done it once. I'll do it again.

    (**JARVIS** *plays.*)

SGT. BURK. *(Pulling gun out.)* That's it clown, put the balloons down and step away from the jungle gym. Now!

DWAYNE. Officer, it wasn't me.

SGT. BURK. Do it, clown! Do it!

(**JARVIS** *plays.* **DWAYNE** *begins making something with balloons.*)

DWAYNE. I'm sorry, Carrie. Honestly, when I first saw you I knew I was lost. I knew somehow you'd kill me. Knew....

PRVT. HANS. Watch him, Burk. What's he making?

(**JARVIS** *plays.*)

DWAYNE. I don't care anymore, Jarvis. It's all over.

SGT. BURK. Clown, stop right there, or...or...I'll fire.

CARRIE. Dwayne, what are you saying? I...I too.... felt something. Don't you know I....

(**CARRIE** *steps between* **DWAYNE** *and* **SGT. BURK.**)

SGT. BURK. Lady move! He's got....

(**DWAYNE** *wields an oversized balloon gun he's just made. Burk and Hans dive and roll for cover.* **JARVIS** *plays and hides behind a tree.*)

SGT. BURK/PRVT. HANS. Gun! Gun! Gun! Gun!

CARRIE. Don't, Dwayne, don't!

SGT. BURK. Lady get out of the way! Get out of the way!

DWAYNE. I love you, Carrie! I love you!

(**DWAYNE** *flees offstage.*)

SGT. BURK. Halt, clown! Halt! Go! Go! Go!

(**HANS** *quickly gives chase.*)

Shoot to kill, Hans! Shoot to kill! *(Beat)* Who do you think you are little lady interfering with police protocol like that?

(**JARVIS** *plays from behind the tree.*)

Get out here, flute boy! Who do you people think you are? Who? You may've jeopardized the arrest of one of the most notorious criminals of our time.

(JARVIS *plays.*)

Wrong. He is not "Dude the Kid Clown." Oh, no, that's an alias. Who would even try and be a "kid clown"? Please, that's just damn pathetic.

CARRIE. Then who is he, officer?

SGT. BURK. Well, Interpol has him listed as the infamously nefarious Jean-Claude Menuisier.

CARRIE. (JARVIS *accompanies her disbelief.*) What?! Impossible, I mean…Who?

(JARVIS *plays.*)

Right. He's "Dude the Kid Clown," not some international Interpol criminal. I mean, he just played at my son's birthday today.

SGT. BURK. Well, for Jean-Claude to be there you must have something he wants. And, wants bad.

(**PRIVATE HANS** *returns dirty and tattered.*)

Report, Private.

PRVT. HANS. Sorry, sir, lost him. He's incredibly quick and agile for a clown. And those big, floppy shoes don't seem to slow him down either. I mean he could be anywhere by now, sir. Anywhere.

SGT. BURK. Right – that's Menuisier for ya. The bastard. Okay, take down their names and numbers and meet me back at H.Q. I've got to get in touch with the Fed's while his trail is still hot.

CARRIE. But, Sergeant, who is this…this Jean-Claude Menu…Menu…?

SGT. BURK. Menuisier. Private, give them a brief brief of the Menuisier file and return A-Sap.

PRVT. HANS. Roger that, sir.

(**SERGEANT BURK** *exits.* **PRIVATE HANS** *quickly, efficiently takes* **CARRIE** *and* **JARVIS***' information.*)

Now, pay attention. You get this once, and only once. Jean-Claude Menuisier, a.k.a. "The Carpenter," is thirty years old and was born in Strasbourg, France. We've not much more personal info than that. He's wanted for espionage and counter-espionage and is linked to the Amsterdam jewel heist of '02, the Barcelona gold debacle of '04, and, most recently, last month's theft of Rodin's "The Thinker." He's believed to have entered the U.S. disguised as a mime from Montreal. If you hear from him give us a call. That's all. Thank you for your cooperation. Good day.

(**PRVT. HANS** *exits on the quick. Beat)*

CARRIE. You know him better than I, could he be this Jean-Claude, "The Carpenter"?

(**JARVIS** *plays.)*

I don't think so either, but…but they sure do.

(**JARVIS** *plays.* **CARRIE** *remains silent.* **JARVIS** *repeats.)*

So what, everyone's got a skeleton, or a mime costume, in their closet, right?

(**JARVIS** *plays.)*

He's not "The Carpenter," okay?

(**JARVIS** *plays.)*

He's just not.

(**JARVIS** *plays.)*

Because…I can tell. He has the tired eyes of a once optimistic man. Of a man looking for a way out, but the world is without doors, or windows. Someone who believed life was fair, was good, was something to be enjoyed, but somewhere along the way discovered the sad, sorrowful truth – life isn't fair. Life is mostly pain, struggle and misunderstanding, and yet, inexplicably, is meant to be enjoyed. That's what I saw in his eyes, Jarvis – a man who has lost hope.

(**JARVIS** *plays a flat, disbelieving question.)*

Yes, from the moment I saw him in that stupid wig with those stupid shoes I loved him. Loved him, for even in his dark oblivion he could continue the struggle, make the attempt, at guiding and directing the children towards joy.

(**JARVIS** *plays a consoling tune.*)

Thank you. The sad thing is I do like Jackie Chan movies and sleeping in on Sundays. Everything. And now….

(**DWAYNE** *enters on the run, missing bright wig and one of his big, floppy shoes.* **JARVIS** *plays in surprise.*)

DWAYNE. Crap on a cracker, those maniacs are serious! They're shooting and everything! I'd no idea my balloon animals were so revolutionarily subversive to threaten The Man. I mean this is crazy.

CARRIE. (**JARVIS** *accompanies* **CARRIE***'s concern.*) Dwayne, are…are you alright?

DWAYNE. Yeah, but I've lost my bright wig, a big, floppy shoe. I need them if I'm going to do Melissa McGrath's party tomorrow.

CARRIE. (**JARVIS** *again accompanies* **CARRIE***.*) Dwayne, forget Melissa McGrath, they think you're Jean-Claude Menuisier, "The Carpenter" – the infamous Interpol thief. They think you crossed the border disguised as a Mime from Montreal, who subsequently….

DWAYNE. One at a time. ONE AT A TIME! PLEASE! Jarvis, what's going on?

(**JARVIS** *plays a long, extended explanation.*)

Carrie, I'm sorry, but…but is there anything you'd like to add?

CARRIE. I'm afraid not.

DWAYNE. You know, I wish I were this Jean-Claude. Because then, maybe, I'd know what to do. Maybe then I'd know I should kiss you and tell you bunny jokes and pull flowers from my sleeve. But I'm not Jean-Claude. I'm Dwayne the once happy-and-jovial but now sad-and-morose Dude the Kid Clown. I'm sorry, Carrie, I have to go.

CARRIE. (JARVIS *accompanies her.*) No, you can't!

DWAYNE. I have to. My hands, these sad digits, can no longer make the animal the children love, want, demand. After this failure I can only become some stupid, pathetic mall clown, or worse yet, a parking lot carnival clown. No, I'm finished. I must leave.

(**JARVIS** *plays something.*)

No, Jarvis. It's too late.

CARRIE. Is it? Why not work for an ad agency? Wear suits and drive a big car? You could get a wife, and a child. You could even....

(**JARVIS** *explains.*)

Exactly. Go undercover.

DWAYNE. And...and on weekends, after slaving and toiling the week away, I could practice making balloon animals.

CARRIE. Yes. Because, eventually, you'll remember how to make your signature animal.

(**JARVIS** *chips in.*)

Right. And, when you do, you'll...you'll be better than ever.

(**DWAYNE** *steps to front of stage and strikes a challenging, commandingly heroic pose.* **JARVIS** *and* **CARRIE** *follow him.*)

DWAYNE. You're right. I can. I can become a copywriter. I can write bright shiny slogans for unnecessary products. I can drive a big, gas guzzling car, have that chef, and...and everything. I can have everything. And...and, while I struggle through the monotonous hours of the daily grind to acquire everything, I will practice. I will practice my balloon animal! I will practice my jokes! My tumbling! My magic! And, eventually, I will persevere! I will persevere until I'm the clown I once was!

(*Lights slowly fade out.*)

End

SKIRMISHES

A SHORT PLAY

CHARACTERS

BRIAN. A young man.
SARAH. A young woman.
FRED. A "formal" ant.
FRANK. A "beach" ant.
GRETA AND GERTRUDE. Female ants dressed as German barmaids.
(Non-speaking roles.)

*(***BRIAN*** *and* ***SARAH*** *are enjoying a picnic downstage right. An eight-foot crumb of French bread sits center stage.* ***FRED***, *dressed in formal wear, enters quietly and hides behind crumb. He makes a phone call on his cell phone, while peering through binoculars at* ***BRIAN*** *and* ***SARAH***.*)

FRED. Western perimeter seems secure, sir. Yeah. Yeah. It's a one-ant job. I got it covered. It looks like…lemon and rosemary roasted chicken, Cajun coleslaw, red potato salad, a Côtes du Rhone, and French bread. No, no baked beans. Yes, sir, I know the queen likes the beans. Could be behind the basket. I'd suggest attacking from the shade of the oak. In one long, thin line. Right. Standard formation. I'll trudge the crumb down A-SAP, sir. Roger. Ten-four. Out.

*(***FRANK***, in beach attire, also with binoculars, enters opposite as* ***FRED*** *prepares to move crumb. They both briefly stretch. Then push with all their might. Nothing. They rotate, in opposite directions, to the other side of the crumb. Both push again. Nothing. They continue the same through* ***BRIAN*** *and* ***SARAH***'s *dialogue.)*

SARAH. Oh, Brian, look at the ants dance.

BRIAN. They're fighting, Sarah. Fighting over a bread-crumb. *(short pause)* Well, they are.

SARAH. Why are you soooo negative?

BRIAN. Because I'm a pessimist.

SARAH. I thought you were an existentialist?

BRIAN. No, that's something an absurdist would say. *(laughs at his joke)* It was a joke.

SARAH. Pass the chicken…please.

(Both ***FRED*** *and* ***FRANK***, *out of breath, step forward on cell phones.)*

FRED.	FRANK.
Sir, yes, it seems to be....	Dude, I thought you said....
One moment, sir.	Dude, a second.

(Finally seeing one another **FRED** *and* **FRANK** *put their phones away. They begin striking martial arts poses.)*

FRED. It seems you've wandered out of your realm.

FRANK. Like the picnic grounds are common territory.

FRED. We sanctioned "lover's hill" and "company barbecue," while you retained "family land" and "parking lot."

FRANK. That was like never formalized, you know? Besides the casualties are too high in family land. Who knew kids could be so sadistic?

FRED. So, you're invading?

FRANK. Dude, you don't "invade" what's rightfully yours. Duh.

FRED. Well, we'll see about that.

FRANK. Bring it on, dude. Bring it on!

FRED. Oh, believe you me, it's going to get brought.

*(***FRED*** *and* ***FRANK*** *begin a stylized ant fight.)*

SARAH. Okay, now they're fighting. Satisfied?

BRIAN. Are you blaming me?

SARAH. We create the world in the vision we want to see.

BRIAN. Is that a yes?

SARAH. I think I preferred you as an existentialist.

BRIAN. Is there more wine?

SARAH. Are you trying to insinuate something?

BRIAN. Yes.

SARAH. That I'm whiney?

BRIAN. That I need another glass of wine. Maybe two.

SARAH. Take the bottle.

BRIAN. Gladly.

*(***FRED*** *and* ***FRANK*** *collapse in a draw.)*

FRED. I'm getting too old for this.

FRANK. You and me both, bro.

SARAH. I think they're dead.

BRIAN. Not surprised.

SARAH. What do you mean by that?

BRIAN. Nothing. Nothing at all.

SARAH. Well, I think it's sad. And all for a breadcrumb.

BRIAN. Men have fought for less.

SARAH. They're you go again being Mr. Pessimist.

BRIAN. It's true. Look at the movie we…Hey, are they moving? I don't think they're dead.

SARAH. What movie, Brian? And don't try and change the subject.

FRED. Do you remember when we ate simply? Berries and nuts and such?

FRANK. Dude, the stuff we collect these days is poison. That Cajun coleslaw? Full of artificial colors and preservatives, and genetically altered cabbage. And what are they putting in the beans? The queen is constantly clamoring for beans, beans, beans!

FRED. Yours too?

FRANK. Dude, like you'd not believe.

FRED. Ours can't get enough either.

FRANK. And when winter rolls around….

(**GRETA** and **GERTRUDE** enter. Each are dressed as German barmaids.)

FRED. Exactly – can't pacify her. Not even Ding Dong wrappers will do. What? What is it?

FRANK. Yo, ladies. Help you with something?

FRED. You cannot touch that crumb. That crumb happens to be for….

FRANK. Dude, chill. Let me handle this. K?

FRED. Yes, but the crumb.

FRANK. The crumb is going nowhere. Trust me. Besides, how often do you find ants dressed as German barmaids? Yow. (**FRANK** *makes an amorous tiger growl.*) Now, ladies, what can we do for you...?

BRIAN. Sarah, check this out. Two other ants have joined the fracas. Though they don't look to be fighting any more....

SARAH. Don't attempt to distract me...I'm brooding.

BRIAN. Now it looks like one's attempting to seduce another one. Though she doesn't seem to be...Aren't ants asexual? I mean....

SARAH. I said, "I'm brooding."

BRIAN. Obviously, being an accountant...and a pessimist, I know nothing about the mating habits of ants, but I'd swear the one has...has basically...bribed? Or would it be bought? Acquired? Acquired the amorous attentions of the one...and....

SARAH. I'M BROODING.

BRIAN. Why, exactly, are you sitting on eggs, dear? *(pause)* Sorry. Not funny. *(short pause)* You're...you're brooding?

SARAH. About you not confiding in me about the movie, which reminded you about the concept of men having gone to war for far less than a crumb of bread.

BRIAN. Oh, that.

SARAH. Yes... *THAT.*

BRIAN. Did we bring a second bottle?

FRED. Half? An entire half of the crumb? You've got to be kidding!

FRANK. They're dressed as German barmaids! They've got accents and everything!

FRED. No. Absolutely not.

FRANK. Dude, don't piss in the hot tub. Please. *(Short pause.)* What were you going to do with the crumb anyway?

FRED. Well.....

FRANK. Exactly. Trudge it over a billion blades of grass, a million miles of blacktop, all the way back to an unappreciative queen who really wants baked beans.

FRED. You've a point.

FRANK. You can have the one with the big antennae….

FRED. Well…okay.

FRANK. Excellent, dude. Excellent. So, ladies….

(FRANK *and* GRETA, FRED *and* GERTRUDE *go to either side of the crumb and make stylized ant love.*)

BRIAN. Sarah, you should see this. I really think they're….

SARAH. Are you talking about *Troy?*

BRIAN. I don't know a Troy. A Tracy, and a….

SARAH. The movie, *Troy,* with Brad Pitt. You think…?

BRIAN. *If* ants are asexual…. Does that mean…they can't have sex, or they can't have offspring? Or….

SARAH. You think women are less than a breadcrumb? Leave the ants alone and answer me. Wow, that is curious.

BRIAN. Isn't it. I guess I was trying to imply – it's easy to find reasons to go to war, a breadcrumb is as good as any, and better than most.

SARAH. Brian, I don't think that's natural.

BRIAN. Of course it is. Agamemnon and Menelaus weren't concerned about Helen. They were concerned about Sparta and Greece's stature. If they allowed Paris to abscond with treasures, Helen being one of them, they'd be dealing with constant raids.

SARAH. Could eating picnic food somehow alter their behavior?

BRIAN. No way. The slaughtering of the Trojans was a foregone conclusion. The concept it was done for "love" was added later, as an excuse. Besides what about sacrificing Iphagenia? Murdering your daughter, so thousands can be lost in battle for one woman. Love? Please. That's stupidity.

SARAH. No, Brian. I meant the ants. I don't think it's natural for them…to be…does that look like it's from the Kama Sutra?

BRIAN. Well. Well. Look at that. Are you taking notes?

SARAH. What do you mean by that? That I need to consult....

BRIAN. No-no-no. Not-at-all. Not-at-all. *(short pause)* I think eating all those baked beans made you edgy.

SARAH. I'm not edgy! And I didn't eat them all!

*(***FRANK** and **GRETA**, **FRED** and **GERTRUDE** *disentangle themselves. All four stretch and prepare to lift the crumb.)*

BRIAN. Well, the container's gone.

SARAH. Are you stupid? Do you really think I ate the container too?

BRIAN. No, but...it...it was right here. Next...next to the basket.

*(***FRED**, **FRANK**, **GRETA**, *and* **GERTRUDE** *exit with the crumb.)*

SARAH. Have some coleslaw instead. And let's watch the ants. They're a fun distraction.

BRIAN. No, no, I'm full. I just want to know what's in those beans.

SARAH. Forget the beans! Here...have a Ding Dong.

End

THE PLAID MAN

A SHORT PLAY

CHARACTERS

DEATH. Dressed all in plaid, including tie and socks. Otherwise he wears black army boots and a black military cap.

CUPID. Dressed in a Hawaiian shirt, shorts and sandals. Her nose is covered in bright zinc cream.

GEORGE. A man dressed in Elizabethan garb.

MARTHA. A woman dressed in Elizabethan garb.

(**DEATH** *and* **CUPID** *sit at a table, there's candlelight and a bottle of wine. Standing, frozen in tableau, in a pool of light, pointing accusatory fingers at one another, are* **GEORGE** *and* **MARTHA.** **DEATH** *snaps his fingers.*)

MARTHA. Thou art an unmuzzled, sheep biting scut.

(**CUPID** *snaps fingers.*)

GEORGE. Why dost thou abuse me so? Surely thou knowest I'm true. True as…as…as…as….

DEATH. It better be good, I've got a doozey for you next.

CUPID. Quiet, please, I'm thinking.

(**DEATH** *snaps fingers.*)

MARTHA. Paunchy, fly-bitten lout.

(**DEATH** *snaps fingers.*)

Rank, onion-eyed pig nut.

(**DEATH** *snaps fingers.*)

Mammering, infectious, fen-sucked coxcomb.

CUPID. I said….

(**CUPID** *snaps fingers.*)

GEORGE. Please, shut up.

DEATH. Here, Cupid, have another glass. Maybe this'll help a little. I thought you were all about love and inspiration?

(**CUPID** *snaps fingers.*)

GEORGE. Shut the frolick up. Please.

(**DEATH** *snaps fingers.*)

MARTHA. Frothy, feted, puking, rump-fed foot-licker.

CUPID. Is that necessary?

DEATH. Yes. Of course.

CUPID. Okay. Got it. (**CUPID** *snaps fingers.*)

GEORGE. Sweet, you know I'm true and constant as the sun's warm rays.

(**DEATH** *snaps fingers.*)

MARTHA. Constant? My eye constant, you goatish cur – the sun disappears every night, every night. Just as you did last Thursday. Oh, indeed I noticed. Indeed I did.

CUPID. Sorry, but isn't the definition of constant....

(**DEATH** *snaps fingers.*)

MARTHA. Who is he, canker-blossom?

CUPID. Um…uh…you realize that's not fair, don't you? Don't you?

DEATH. Hey, I'm the Grim-frigging-Reaper, remember? I know all about fair and unfair, don't I?

CUPID. Oh, here we go again. Soapbox time.

DEATH. Cupid, what, realistically, is fair? Is it fair to be born into the privileged class and country instead of months premature to a third world, crack mother? Is it fair a twelve-year-old dies of a bee sting and a serial killer lives to ninety? No, it's not. Therefore.... (**DEATH** *snaps fingers.*)

MARTHA. Who is he, maggot pie?

CUPID. I thought I said that's not fair? Besides you know what I mean.

(**DEATH** *snaps fingers.*)

MARTHA. Who is he, wagtail?

CUPID. Death, please, give me a moment. Some things do take time.

DEATH. You know I prefer, Grim. I'd like to think I've outgrown Death – even if you don't believe it. Death seems so Dark Age-ish, plague and witchcraft riddled. Bring out your dead, bring out your dead…you know? And, don't get me started on Time. Okay?

CUPID. Heaven forbid we'd be here for eons. But, regardless, Death, it's not fair for you to....

(**DEATH**, *about to snap fingers, is pre-empted by* **CUPID**'s *furious flurry of snaps.* **GEORGE** *takes a deep breath....*)

GEORGE. Turtle dove-love I love you like no other not even the world sun and moon can diminish your beauty I bask in only increases my desire to make your happiness my life to cherish and honor and respect beyond all others without fail or question anything you say or do to spend the rest of our live long days together joyous in beautiful bountiful love is what I am with you fair damsel of desire and wonder at how lucky I am to be with you makes me so very very happy sometimes your beauty and our love feels as if it's going to cause me to....

(**GEORGE** *faints.*)

DEATH. Impressive.

CUPID. Thanks, Grim, I'll take that as a compliment. So, is everything okay? You seem...distracted tonight. Or, more correctly, looking for a fight.

(**DEATH** *snaps fingers.*)

MARTHA. Consciousness is simply "a being such that in its being, its being is in question in so far as this being implies a being other than itself."

CUPID. Like I said, looking for a fight. It's not necessary to bring in French existentialism, is it?

(**DEATH** *snaps fingers.*)

MARTHA. Or, more succinctly, "Consciousness is a being, the nature of which is to be conscious of the nothingness of its being."

CUPID. Somehow, you know, that's very sad.

DEATH. That's Jean-Paul Sartre. That's French existentialism.

CUPID. Okay, what's wrong?

DEATH. Nothing.

CUPID. Is it St. Peter, again? Rattling his keys about how it's your fault he's so busy?

DEATH. That winy punk has nothing to do with it. Okay? Trust me.

CUPID. Then what?

DEATH. It's nothing. Honest.

CUPID. Grim, I can tell something's bothering you. Come on, what is it?

DEATH. I said it was nothing. Okay? Can we just get on with this?

CUPID. Sure. If that's how you want to play. I must be mistaken, thinking we're closer than that.

DEATH. It's not that. It's just....

(**CUPID** *snaps fingers.*)

GEORGE. Honey, let's make up. There is no one else. Honest. Okay?

DEATH. Cupid, look.... It's just....

(**CUPID** *snaps fingers.*)

GEORGE. You mean the world to me. Honest. Okay?

DEATH. Don't be like this, Cupe. Please....

(**CUPID** *snaps fingers.*)

GEORGE. Without you I can't go on. Honest.

DEATH. Fine. (**DEATH** *snaps fingers.*)

MARTHA. Honey, you rock my world.

(**CUPID** *snaps fingers.*)

GEORGE. Your depressed demeanor sends shivers up and down my spine.

(**DEATH** *snaps fingers.*)

MARTHA. Oh, sorry, stallion of mine, I meant you're prissy and high-maintenance.

CUPID. Excuse me? (**CUPID** *snaps fingers.*)

GEORGE. You're crude, vile, despicable and smell exactly like frog warts and bat wings.

(**DEATH** *snaps fingers.*)

MARTHA. You look like a cadaver in red.

(**CUPID** *snaps fingers.*)

GEORGE. Plaid gives you a healthy glow.

(**DEATH** *snaps fingers.*)

MARTHA. I never had an orgasm.

(**CUPID** *snaps fingers.*)

GEORGE. Neither did I.

(**DEATH** *snaps fingers.*)

MARTHA. Did too.

(**CUPID** *snaps fingers.*)

GEORGE. Did not.

(**DEATH** *snaps fingers.*)

MARTHA. Did too!

(**CUPID** *snaps fingers.*)

GEORGE. Did not!

(*Both* **CUPID** *and* **DEATH** *snap fingers in rapid succession.*)

MARTHA.	GEORGE.
I don't know how this fiasco of friendship ever got started with a demi-god of such little consequence and import that the dregs of society call queen of the toilet so you and the horse you rode in on can flit back to the cherry orchard of heart shaped lies which only idiots call home is where you should go wallow and stew in the sour noxious fumes of your pathetic hypocritical hackneyed happiness.	It's inconceivable how a scowling dork with the mind of a radish and the personality of a toadstool can gaze in a mirror without throwing up every pathetic scrap of their inconsequential being which is a loathing dank twisted rabid fetid figure and is a pox and plague upon the entire galaxy and should probably stick to something they're qualified for like picking up dog poop.

(MARTHA and GEORGE collapse. DEATH and CUPID snap fingers. MARTHA and GEORGE twitch in response. Beat.)

CUPID. Grim, I'm sorry. I know how hard it is for you to open up. I should be more understanding, a little more patient.

DEATH. Cupe, it's not you, it's me. I let work affect and undermine our friendship. But, damn it, it's not easy being "The Grim Reaper," you know? Sometimes, after a century of plague, a decade of war and famine, I want someone else to take the first step. Of course it's a power thing. The fear of being vulnerable, of intimacy, of…But…the rational is not ruler to the emotional, you know?

CUPID. All too well – I'm Cupid, remember?

DEATH. Preaching to the choir, eh?

CUPID. Yep. Why don't we try and start over?

(CUPID snaps fingers. GEORGE sits up.)

GEORGE. I want to love you. I want to love you to the bottom of the sea.

(CUPID snaps fingers.)

Drowning, I cannot give or take. Yes, your eyes are that deep.

CUPID. What, no snide remark? No…. *(CUPID snaps fingers.)*

GEORGE. Bawdy, wayward, yeasty half-faced strumpet.

CUPID. Grim, you okay? Too much wine? You want some water? Grim, I know exactly what you were saying. I do the same thing. Everybody does. It's okay. Instead how about we….

DEATH. Look, I thought we were going to get together and have a good time. Kind of the same old same old, you know?

CUPID. What…what do you mean?

DEATH. I thought we'd…. *(DEATH snaps fingers.)*

MARTHA. Get out and away from the sad formalities which constrain our attempt at creating some meaningful reason for doing what we're doing. I want to enjoy us without worrying about the consequences, or the ramifications, of being with you, because…because we're all going to die sometime, right?

(**MARTHA** *kisses* **GEORGE** *on the cheek.*)

CUPID. Did…did you mean that?

DEATH. About us dying?

CUPID. No, about….

(**CUPID** *snaps fingers.* **GEORGE** *kisses* **MARTHA** *on cheek.*)

DEATH. Did you mean…? (**DEATH** *snaps fingers.*)

MARTHA. I want to love you madly – to the bottom of the sea. Yes, your eyes are that deep.

CUPID. Grim? You really are afraid, aren't you?

DEATH. I thought it was going to be like we've done before. You know? Hang out. Just…casual. Beer, pool and… and casual, you know? But this? Something's changed. Somehow…something's changed.

(**DEATH** *snaps fingers.* **MARTHA** *again kisses* **GEORGE.**)

You know?

CUPID. Yes, I think so. But…but, Grim…I thought…? So, you meant it?

(**DEATH** *snaps fingers.* **MARTHA** *again kisses* **GEORGE.** *However, this time they continue and progress in their affections.*)

DEATH. It must be some mid-existence crisis. Lately I've had the realization no one likes me. I'm always, and I mean always, the bad guy. No one ever wants to be around me, unless they're a suicide bomber. And they don't count. They're real assholes. St. Peter's got nothing on them.

CUPID. You realize, I hope, I don't think that way of you, don't you?

DEATH. As a suicide bomber, as an asshole?

CUPID. No. As not liking you.

DEATH. Yes, of course. Regardless of all our... *(feigns snapping fingers.)* But....

CUPID. What? Tell me. Please.

DEATH. Well...when I'm wandering the mortal plain, striking and shuddering souls from their flesh, I can't help but think of you. My mind wanders and...and I don't know why I'm doing what I'm doing. Everything seems surreal and absurd without you. Everything.

CUPID. Grim, that's...Wow.

DEATH. Holy cow.

> *(*DEATH *and* CUPID *snap fingers.* MARTHA *and* GEORGE *disentangle, stand and dust themselves off.* DEATH *snaps fingers.)*

MARTHA. What do we do now?

> *(*CUPID *snaps fingers.)*

GEORGE. I...I don't know.

> *(*CUPID *snaps fingers.)*

> What do we do now?

> *(*DEATH *snaps fingers.)*

MARTHA. I don't know.

CUPID. So, you really meant...? *(*CUPID *snaps fingers.)*

GEORGE. Everything seems surreal and absurd without you.

DEATH. Yes. And, I meant.... *(*DEATH *snaps fingers.)*

MARTHA. I want to love you to the bottom of the sea. Drowning, I cannot give or take. Yes, your eyes are that deep.

CUPID. I said that.

DEATH. Oh, right, right, right. Sorry.

> *(*CUPID *snaps fingers.)*

GEORGE. Tell me yourself. I want to hear you say it.

DEATH. W-what?

(**CUPID** *snaps fingers.*)

GEORGE. Tell me yourself. I want to hear you say it.

DEATH. I…I love you.

(**CUPID** *snaps fingers.*)

GEORGE. Say it again.

DEATH. I love you. (**DEATH** *snaps fingers.*)

MARTHA. Well…say something.

CUPID. I love you, too. (**CUPID** *snaps fingers.*)

GEORGE. Kiss me.

DEATH. Gladly.

(**DEATH** *and* **CUPID** *kiss. While they embrace they snap fingers.*)

MARTHA/GEORGE. Waiter? Check please!

End

NORTH POLE WINTER WOES

A SHORT PLAY

CHARACTERS

SANTA. The gift giving man of the North Pole.
SAM. A bartender.
VERN. An Elf.

(A neighborhood bar in the North Pole, in the back-ground Tom Waits plays, perhaps The Piano's Drunk, Not Me. **SANTA** *sits nursing a beer as* **SAM** *cleans the bar.)*

SANTA. Rather ironic – sad really – that we know nothing of the way the universe is today, don't you think so, Sam?

SAM. Santa, that's not an acceptable topic of conversation – you know that.

SANTA. I know that monstrous money pit in the sky – I of course refer to the Hubble telescope – only gazes into the far reaches of the past.

SAM. Santa, please.

SANTA. But imagine where we would be if it were able to see into the future. Just imagine, Sam. Just imagine.

SAM. Ya know, Santa, it being nearly Christmas and all, maybe you should keep the philosophy to yourself? Okay? I don't need anymore fights like the other night. Okay?

SANTA. Very well, Sam. However, you realize, it was not "philosophy" which instigated that fruckus, but sheer ignorance and bigotry. I was well within my rights to point out the hypocrisy of those leftwing labor….

SAM. Santa, drop it. You're preaching to the choir. Besides I can't afford another "fruckus," so keep your pessimistic rhetoric to yourself. Please?

SANTA. Well, philosophically speaking, Sam, if I were a pessimist, children would be getting avian flu vaccinations and radiation suits.

SAM. And why aren't they?

SANTA. Because elves are afraid of flying and formal wear.

*(***VERN*** *enters.)*

VERN. Where is he? Where is that pudgy, no good, two timing bastard? Sam! Where is that fat son-of-a-Ho-Ho-Ho?

SAM. Still haven't got those glasses yet, eh, Vern?

VERN. Hell no, you know our health care is bullshit. But cut the chit-chat, where is he?

SAM. Two chairs to your left. And you keep it friendly, otherwise....

VERN. Sure, Sam. Sure. Okay, chub-master, prepare for the ass whoopin' of your life.

SANTA. Your other left, Vern. He'll be okay, Sam. Relax.

SAM. He better be.

SANTA. Closer. Closer. Almost....

SAM. Shut up, fat man. I don't need your help.

(**VERN** *wanders away.*)

SANTA. Sam, would you be kind enough to redirect our friend?

SAM. This is ridiculous.

SANTA. Ah, what aspect of life isn't? I think Camus once said something to the extent that given the choice between existence and....

SAM. What'd I say, Santa?

VERN. Is he still philosophizing?

SAM. Give him a pint and what else does he want to do?

VERN. Besides play with his candy cane?

SANTA. Ignorance, my friends, is not armor, or an excuse.

SAM. Tell it to Jack Frost, Santa. There ya go, Vern – the pudgy one is at twelve o'clock.

VERN. Thanks, Sam. Okay, blubber boots, prepare for the ass whoopin' of a lifetime.

SANTA. One moment, Vern, before you "whoop my ass," would you please tell me what this is about?

VERN. Hey, jelly belly, you know damn well this is about Clarese.

SANTA. I'm sorry, Vern, but who is Clarese?

VERN. You rosy cheeked rapscallion you don't even remember her name! She's my wife!

SANTA. I'm sorry, Vern, I didn't know you were married.

VERN. You were best man at my wedding!

SANTA. I'm best man at every elf's wedding, Vern. You can't realistically expect me to remember every elf that gets married and their wives too. Can you?

SAM. Hey, Santa, what about all the world's kids?

VERN. Yeah, ya fur lined fridge, what about all those kids?

SANTA. A unique affliction which makes me Santa and has tormented me all my life, thank you very much.

VERN. Yeah, well, every elf I've talked to has….

SANTA. Vern, tales of my philandering are greatly exaggerated. Greatly. Even the reindeer repeat the same sordid stories – and do you believe them?

VERN. Well, no. Donner and Blitzen have always blamed you for Rudolph getting top billing. They've even mentioned….

SANTA. Look I left the bar well after Rudolph. Sure we had a few drinks. Sure we see one another outside of work, but so what? He and I are close friends, nothing more. Okay?

VERN. Sure, Santa. Sure.

SANTA. Would you care to add anything, Sam?

SAM. Uh, no. No thank you.

SANTA. All these tall tales are mere attempts by a few left-wing hot-heads to undermine my credibility. I'm an easy target – a responsible, upstanding authority figure. Besides, who are you going to finger in a police line-up, a middle-age man in a drab suit and tie, or the jolly, fat man in the bright, red suit?

SAM/VERN. Fat man in the red suit.

SANTA. And that's exactly what I've been saying. It's simply a form of profiling. I'm surprised I haven't been blamed for more unsavory incidences than bedding a few wives in the toy room.

VERN. How did you know Clarese said it was the toy room?! Ass whoopin' time!

SANTA. Vern! All the supposed wives get it supposedly in the toy room – it's a double entendre.

VERN. That's disgusting.

SANTA. Vern, will you shut up and sit down and have a beer with me?

VERN. No. I am going to kick your ass.

SANTA. *(taking out a small gift box)* At least open this first. It should help you with my "ass whooping."

VERN. What…what is it?

SANTA. It looks like a Christmas present, doesn't it, Sam?

SAM. Sure does, Santa. Sure does.

VERN. For me? Is this a bribe? Hush money? Because if you think I'm not going to whoop your ass, you've got another thing coming – like a double ass whooping.

SANTA. Oh, my God, will you just shut up and open the stupid thing? Sam, please, another round.

SAM. You got it, Santa.

(VERN pulls a pair of glasses out of the box.)

VERN. Santa…Santa these…these are perfect. Right size. Right prescription. How…how'd you know?

SANTA. Uh, because I'm, Santa? Vern, if I wanted, I could pull a walrus out of my ass. Shut up Sam.

VERN. Santa….wow, Santa. They're even Italian.

SANTA. Well, Vern, I feel my elves deserve the best.

VERN. YOUR elves? YOUR elves?

SANTA. Look, Vern, that's not….

VERN. Shit, the Elvin workshop is just a glitzy plantation for you, isn't it? Yes, Masta Santa. Right away, Masta Santa. While you just sit on your high-flying sled reaping the rewards and getting fat and jolly on our labor.

SANTA. Vern, if I were given a moment to explain….

VERN. Explain what? Explain that a pale power-player has exploited an indigenous populace for too long? Has genetically manipulated the local fauna so they can talk and fly and…who knows what else for his sadistic pleasures.

SANTA. Please Vern, you know as well as I the Island of Misbegotten Toys is an anarchist/insurgent stronghold vowed to bring the North Pole under fascist rule and has nothing to do with my theoretical "sadistic pleasures."

VERN. Says you – black boot booty boy – and your PR zombies, the penguins.

SANTA. Penguins can't lie, Vern. Why do you think they can slide on their bellies?

(Beat as **VERN** *ponders. Finally…)*

VERN. Because, anatomically, through years of evolution, a thick layer of fat has built up to assist in their propulsion across the frigid surface. I might even hazard the skin on their bellies is less sensitive. So for you to use that as an example of their honesty simply underlines your manipulative nature, Jolly Mick Jerk-off. Wow, these glasses really work.

SAM. Sounds pretty probable to me, Santa.

SANTA. Sam?

SAM. Yeah?

SANTA. Shut up. Please.

SAM. Uh, okay.

VERN. Oh, I see everything clearly now, puddin' paunch. The glasses, the pint, the feigned friendliness – all an attempted, sweet, little seduction, yeah? But I got you're number. You're all about the rosy cheeks, the red suit, the sincere "Ho-Ho-Ho" – but its gloss. It's all part of the "Santa Seduction Package." How else would those naïve kids leave their cookies and milk out? Well, seduce this, tapioca tummy.

*(***SANTA*** *receives an "ass whoopin'" from* **VERN***. It is done in slow motion with* **VERN** *occasionally adding commentary.)*

POW! To your lying kisser! KA-THUD! To your smelty kidney! WA-THWACK! To the paunchy small of your back! BA-CHUNCK! To your fat funk! KA-BLASST! To your lying, conniving ass! I'll see you on the picket lines, mistletoe dick.

(VERN gives one last kick to SANTA and exits. SANTA is splayed on his back, panting. SAM watches, mildly amused.)

SAM. Santa? Santa you okay?

SANTA. Jesus, I am going to have distribution problems this year.

SAM. You're okay though? Right?

SANTA. Yeah, I'm okay. It's nothing another pint won't alleviate.

SAM. Okay, but shouldn't you be getting back to the missus?

SANTA. Who do you think has been escorting the wives to the toy room?

SAM. Honestly? I thought it was that stupid, mustachioed, singing snowman.

SANTA. As did I, Sam. As did I. Then one afternoon...well, the veil was lifted and the missus has been feeding me high fat, high cholesterol entrees on some premise "it assists my jollyness" – conniving, little bitch.

SAM. How do you think that snowman glides so smoothly? I mean, that's cool. That's something I wish I could do. I've tried...but....

SANTA. Yeah, well, the missus best not run into the Abominable Snowmonster alone on the icepack. He and I? Let's just say we've an understanding, okay?

SAM. Sure thing, Santa. Besides, you know me – Silence is my middle name.

SANTA. Yes, it is, Sam. Yes, it is.

(They laugh briefly together. SAM moves off as SANTA takes a cell phone out and dials.)

SANTA. *(continued)* Hey, Rudolph, what're doing tonight? Thought we might gaze upon the stars and ponder the cosmos. Well, it's my understanding the best viewing is at the Island of Misbegotten Toys. Exactly. I'll meet you there.

*(**SANTA** starts his standard jolly chuckle which, as the lights descend, grows into a malevolent cackle.)*

End

THE ABDUCTION

A SHORT-SHORT PLAY

CHARACTERS

DAWN. A young woman.
CHRIS. A young man.

(A warm summer evening in the middle of a large field. **DAWN** *and* **CHRIS** *lie on folding plastic lounge chairs counting meteors. Between them is a cooler filled with beer and a fifth of Tequila. It's obvious they've been there for some time. Initially all that can be heard is the sound of crickets and a slight breeze.)*

DAWN. Eighteen.

*(***CHRIS*** takes a small shot of tequila and a sip of beer. Beat.)*

CHRIS. Nineteen. And twenty. Right, back at you.

DAWN. No way. No way.

CHRIS. Yeah, baby. Drink it and weep.

DAWN. Where, asshole, where?

CHRIS. Moving left to right, out of Cassiopeia. Nineteen and twenty. Drink.

DAWN. God, I hate you. *(***DAWN*** takes a small shot of tequila and a sip of beer.)* Asshole. *(beat)* So, where's Cassiopeia?

CHRIS. Big dipper. Two middle stars. Follow them out, left to right. The series of stars that look like a 'W', that's Cassiopeia.

DAWN. Okay. Got it. *(beat)* So, when do we get abducted? Not to imply I don't want to, I do, it's just that it's getting a little chilly and I've got work in the morning.

CHRIS. Well, the majority occur between 11:15 and midnight.

DAWN. What you're an expert or something?

CHRIS. Yeah, you could say it falls under the "or something" category – an occupational hobby.

DAWN. What's with the mys…. Twenty-two! Twenty-two! Yeah, right back at you! Baby!

*(***CHRIS*** drinks.)*

CHRIS. Uh, you know of course I let you have that, right?

DAWN. So, why'd you come back?

CHRIS. Why'd you never leave?

DAWN. Who says I didn't?

CHRIS. Good point. Did you?

DAWN. Twenty-three. Twenty-three.

(**CHRIS** *drinks.*)

Damn, this is amazing. I've never seen so many shooting stars...ever. And, I mean ever.

CHRIS. I...I believe you.

DAWN. Good. *(beat)* Chris?

CHRIS. Yeah?

DAWN. I'm glad you're here. What I'm trying to say... well....

CHRIS. I know, Dawn. I know.

DAWN. So, tell me, how long are you in town for?

CHRIS. Not long.

DAWN. Why?

CHRIS. Because.

DAWN. That, Mr. Mystery, tells me absolutely, positively nothing.

CHRIS. Okay, how about this...I'm in town because my father was diagnosed with advanced prostate cancer. I leave when he's dead. The doctors gave me a six to eight month residency. How's that for an answer?

DAWN. Chris, I'm sorry, I didn't know.

CHRIS. That's okay. It's over.

DAWN. And, thank you, that does answer some things. *(beat)* Chris, we're alone, aren't we?

CHRIS. Ten minute walk into Prosser's field, I should think so.

DAWN. No. I meant.... *(beat)* I meant here, as on Earth, alone, in the galaxy, in the cosmos.

CHRIS. You asking me personally, or as an astrophysicist?

DAWN. Excuse me?

CHRIS. Twenty-four.

DAWN. What?

CHRIS. Twenty-four.

DAWN. Answer the question.

CHRIS. I did. Twenty….

DAWN. No, no, about you being an…an astrophysicist.

CHRIS. Twenty-four. *(beat)* You're not drinking. *(beat)*

DAWN. Fine. There. Satisfied?

CHRIS. Gosh, Superwoman, sure am. You know, you're amazing. Can you leap tall buildings, too?

DAWN. Bite me. *(beat)* Asshole. *(beat)*

CHRIS. So, everyone seems to think.

DAWN. And, what do you mean by that?

CHRIS. Nothing.

DAWN. Sure. So, are we going to be able to find our way back? I mean, we didn't bring a flashlight and…. *(beat)* I mean…it…it was sunset.

CHRIS. Yeah, we'll be fine.

DAWN. Yeah?

CHRIS. Oh, yeah. Not a problem. If need be we can just follow the trampled grass. No big deal at all. *(beat)* You alright?

DAWN. No.

CHRIS. Oh. *(beat)* Something I said, or you drank?

DAWN. Neither.

CHRIS. Oh. *(beat)* I'll take that one. **(CHRIS** *drinks.)* You know the story of Cassiopeia is rather interesting. Seems she was Queen to the King of….

DAWN. Chris?

CHRIS. Yeah?

DAWN. Shut up.

CHRIS. Uh…okay. *(beat)* You know, I'm absolutely sure we can get out of here. We just need to follow the path through the grass. Shouldn't be a problem at all. I mean….

DAWN. Chris?

CHRIS. Uh...shut up?

DAWN. Yeah. *(Beat. Beat. Double beat.)* I love you.

CHRIS. Yeah, yeah, I can see how...how you'd love the... the stars?

DAWN. No.

CHRIS. The...the crickets? The mesmerizing melody of the crickets?

DAWN. No.

CHRIS. The fragrant, gentle breeze wafting delicately across the wild flowers?

DAWN. No.

CHRIS. Oh. *(Beat. Beat.)* Dawn, I'm sure it's just the beer, or more probably the te-kill-ya, but....

DAWN. Chris, shut up.

CHRIS. Right. Okay. Shutting up.... Now.

DAWN. Why do you think I agreed to be abducted? *(beat)* Uh, Chris?

CHRIS. Oh, sorry, didn't know speech had been returned. Sorry. Uh, for the beer?

DAWN. No, asshole. Because of that night on the hood of your parents' car. Remember?

CHRIS. Of course.

DAWN. We were like ten, or so. We stared at the stars for hours and hours and just talked. Talked until our parents had to yell at us to come inside. Anyway, I think that was the first time you told me about that lump in your neck. About you believing you were some alien recording device and they'd eventually come and collect you. Remember?

CHRIS. Uh, unfortunately, yes. *(beat)* Why?

DAWN. Because that's when...when I knew I loved you. I know we were just kids, but I thought it was the funniest, sweetest, dearest thing and...and I still do.

CHRIS. Dawn?

DAWN. No. Let me finish.

CHRIS. Okay. *(beat)*

DAWN. When you and your parents moved I cried for weeks. Literally weeks. Mom kept asking what was wrong, and I simply told her some stupid lie about some girl pulling my hair in recess.

CHRIS. Jenny Fuller?

DAWN. Yeah, I mean she was a stuck-up bitch and deserved it, but....

CHRIS. No, she was a babe. And she wasn't going to allow no other chicas – like yourself – to rustle men off her pretty, pretty babe ranch without some kind of a tussle. Yeah?

DAWN. God, will you shut up? *(beat)* Anyway, I never thought I'd see you again. Never thought I'd have the opportunity to.... Oh, twenty-four. Twenty-four.

*(**CHRIS** doesn't drink.)*

Hey, mister, I said twenty-four. Chris, I.... Why's it getting bigger?

CHRIS. Remember what I said?

DAWN. About what?

CHRIS. My dad.

DAWN. Yeah. You know this one's not...not....

CHRIS. Burning up?

DAWN. Right. It kind of looks like....

CHRIS. My dad died yesterday and....

DAWN. ...Like it's coming right for us.

CHRIS. See, that's just it. That thing in my neck, well..... I love you, too.

(The field is engulfed in bright lights, the whir and rumble of light speed engines. Instantly the stage goes dark.)

End

NATURAL SELECTION

A SHORT PLAY

CHARACTERS

MOTHER HUNGER. A garish soccer mom.
MOTHER DESIRE. A garish soccer mom.
MOTHER PERFECTION. A refined soccer mom.

(A soccer park. **MOTHER HUNGER** *and* **MOTHER DESIRE** *stand watching a game.)*

DESIRE. Don't you just love watching children play?

HUNGER. So, innocent. So, carefree.

DESIRE. Like bunnies bounding in a field.

HUNGER. Fawns frolicking in a meadow. *(beat)*

DESIRE. And then something happens.

HUNGER. *(As Mother Hunger's mother.)* Wendy, damn it, how many times have I told you no mashed potatoes for Grandpa? You call that a skirt? Then walk, I don't have time to drive you all over Eternity. I don't care just don't get pregnant! *(beat)* Yes. And then something happens.

DESIRE. *(As Mother Desire's mother.)* Jenny, are those earrings? Didn't I say not until you were eight? Next thing you know you'll be dating the basketball team and moving to Chicago. And don't think I don't notice how you hold your school books and the grades you get! Smart? Smart like a slutty, slut-slut! *(beat)* And then something happens. *(beat)*

HUNGER. It's really too bad.

DESIRE. It is. It, really, is. Bunnies end up as key chains.

HUNGER. And fawns end up on the walls of cabins. *(beat)*

DESIRE. So, which one's yours?

HUNGER. He's the cute tyke with the mullet wearing the skull and cross-bones T-shirt.

DESIRE. With the steel toed boots and strong arming the others for their candy?

HUNGER. That's him – Little Big Bill. Third string goalie.

DESIRE. Good technique, at least for acquiring candy.

HUNGER. A mingling of Aikido and Jujitsu. Though tweaking the thumb…right there…like that…all his. A Picasso of pain, if you will.

DESIRE. Yes, however, he seems….

HUNGER. Billy! Damn it, you don't take from the girls! Give to the girls! Give to the girls! Remember what I told you about blow jobs and meaningless sex?! Okay! Take from the weak and give to the trollops! That's a good boy! *(beat)* Kids these days.

DESIRE. So hard to train; unless, of course, you've a soundproof room, a cattle prod, and a sander.

HUNGER. Billy always was a bit greedy. When he was nursing we practically needed a bouncer to keep him off my tit.

DESIRE. Even from here I can tell he has your dark, untrusting, and carnivorous eyes.

HUNGER. Doesn't he though? First, we likened them to a fox's, and then a wolf's, but, after he ate his way through his crib, we settled on a badger.

DESIRE. You know, I…I can see a bit of badger in yours.

HUNGER. Thank you. But he really takes after his father – an ex-Enron executive. And, which little one is yours?

DESIRE. He's the one kicking knees and breaking ankles out at midfield.

HUNGER. He's a solid looking boy, isn't he? Fast too.

DESIRE. Yes, the steroid treatments are finally starting to take effect.

HUNGER. But…what about the anger and the acne?

DESIRE. Cattle prod and a palm sander.

HUNGER. That'd explain the Phantom of the Opera smile.

DESIRE. Yes, we're hoping by the sixth grade to have him sign with Nike, or Adidas.

HUNGER. So, therefore, looks and personality won't matter. He'll be able to afford a sleek, silicon runway model.

DESIRE. Honestly, his father and I would prefer a liposuctioned, tummy-tucked, Hollywood queen of Botox rather than an anorexic, car-crash-in-high-heels, heroin addict.

HUNGER. You sound a bit like my hair plugged, Viagra popping husband.

DESIRE. And once puberty hits we'll have his eyes laser adjusted.

HUNGER. You mean like Mark McGuire's?

DESIRE. Yes, but instead of 20-10, we're hoping for 10-10, or even 5-5. We looked into transplants, but they're only doing internal organs presently. Hopefully, with his children they can perhaps insert peregrine eyes. *(beat)* Jeremy! Don't help him up! Check the ref, and kick him again if you can get away with it! Young man, you do not talk back to me!

*(**MOTHER DESIRE** makes the sound and movement of using a cattle prod and sander.)*

That's my boy. That's my ego-starved little lumpkin. That's it. That's it. Easy…easy. Now! Now! Return to the kill! Return! *(beat)* See what I mean? Give me a sound proof room and a cattle prod and I'll give you a goddamn saint.

HUNGER. You know, I couldn't agree more. I know I sure wish my mother would've been more of a raging, lunatic bitch with a penchant for cross-eyed sadomasochism and the foresight to have a doctor inject me with mysterious concoctions, or even use searing electrical devices to keep me from squandering my youth through enjoyment and self-discovery.

DESIRE. It sure would've saved a lot of time.

HUNGER. You're telling me. If I'd known I could get a West Hills house, a German sedan, and a maid all for the low, low price of two missionary positions, a blow job, and a "Yes! Yes! Yes, you're a Greek god of Love!" once a week, I don't know what I would've done with my life after sixteen.

DESIRE. Exactly. Instead, what'd we do with our youth?

HUNGER. Go bowling and laugh at the pale, chicken legs of old men being swallowed by argyle socks, while drinking tin can beer.

DESIRE. Go to second base beneath the brilliant, summer stars on the 8th hole of the Languedoc Country Club with a nervous, shy boy named Chris.

HUNGER. Foolish.

DESIRE. Stupid – his hands were freezing.

(**MOTHER PERFECTION** *enters and stands to one side.*)

DESIRE. Do you know that friendly, well meaning bitch?

HUNGER. Oh, I've seen her plenty of times stopping at crosswalks and yellow lights. I hate her.

DESIRE. Yeah, well, I've already a list of assassins to make a hit on her son if he plays the same position as mine in junior high.

HUNGER. You're kidding. Are they expensive?

DESIRE. Actually, most are surprisingly reasonable. And, usually, for a few thousand more you can have them make it appear like a suicide, a mafia hit, a government cover-up, or an alien abduction.

(**MOTHER PERFECTION** *waves to the other Mothers – they disdain.*)

DESIRE. Bitch.

HUNGER. Slut. *(beat)* So, which runny nosed, piss ant, conniving brat is hers?

DESIRE. That one. *(beat)*

HUNGER. But…but…that's…that's im-impossible.

DESIRE. Isn't it? *(beat)* Now you know it's not a legend. Simply a sick, disgusting and disturbing fact.

HUNGER. Yes, but…but….

DESIRE. In the first trimester they say she gave him Beethoven, Brahms, Bach, Mozart, whole grains, organic vegetables, free range proteins, exercise and, most disturbing of all, sincere love.

HUNGER. Disgust me. What about 'weight-gain-resentment'?

DESIRE. No. Nothing. Instead of blaming the child, she accepted everything, even swollen ankles, hemorrhoids, and diarrhea, benevolently. I, personally – and this is just me talking – fucking hate her.

HUNGER. I'll bet her parent's said they loved her – and meant it.

DESIRE. No doubt. The father, if you can imagine, even swore his fidelity and desire for the child – regardless (so he claimed) what the ultrasound exposed of the fetus.

HUNGER. B-before the doctors had confirmed it didn't have three heads, dragon wings, and a thirst for the blood of Scientologists?

DESIRE. Yes.

HUNGER. Incredible.

DESIRE. Disgusting is more like it.

HUNGER. He had to be on medication?

DESIRE. No. Theoretically…neither of them were. *(beat)*

HUNGER. How is it possible for a child to be so beautiful?

DESIRE. He's a lithe, lean god.

HUNGER. See how he runs? Are…are those golden sparks exploding from beneath his heels?

DESIRE. The ball is struck, and struck so true it sings Ave Maria into the back of the net.

HUNGER. Look how he congratulates his teammates – genuinely – without a snide comment, or gesture, to the little, pathetic – losers! Yes, I'm talking about you, Jeremy! Stop pouting and get back there and kick some ass! I don't care if you don't feel like it! What has Mr. Electrical-Shock taught you about obeying mother?

(She again feigns use and sounds of cattle prod and sander.)

Exactly. Now get back there.

DESIRE. We've obtained blood and stool samples and he checks out clean.

HUNGER. Impossible. Look at that smile. If not Prozac, or Paxil, or Percodan, or Zoloft, or St. John's Wort, at least mint flavored whitening strips.

DESIRE. He is rather...rather mesmerizing to watch...isn't he?

HUNGER. Yes, but let's see if little Jeremy might even things by cracking an ankle, or shattering a knee.

DESIRE. There's nothing like the sweet elixir of vindictive pain to heal old, ignorant wounds.

PERFECTION. Uh...um...excuse me. Is...is that your boy out there?

HUNGER. The one running headlong through the fray? The one scattering carnage in his wake and attempting to dislodge a joint, or limb?

PERFECTION. Yes, he's the one.

HUNGER. I do accept that he exited my loins, though how he got there...I confess complete ignorance.

PERFECTION. Well...he seems to play rather rough.

DESIRE. The first law of the jungle gym, my dear, is the strong shall survive, and the weak shall drink lattes and read.

PERFECTION. Laws are arbitrary contrivances. Once one is a god laws become obsolete.

HUNGER. Even off-sides? What about red cards?

PERFECTION. The parameters become entrenched within one's beatific nature. Here and There are simply redefined as Everywhere.

DESIRE. Billy! Stop pilfering candy and go kick the shit out of that little angelic ass over there!

PERFECTION. Violence is simply a reflection of one's own ignorance.

HUNGER. While you were pregnant you probably didn't even drink alcohol, eat processed sugar, or masturbate.

PERFECTION. I will confess one night, late in the summer, the heat was so oppressive I couldn't sleep and I….

DESIRE. Had two bags of barbecue flavored potato chips, a half-gallon of Neapolitan ice cream, a pack of Oreos, a dozen crispy Kosher pickles, a spicy Slim Jim all washed down with a six-pack of Kaiser pilsners while watching a South Park marathon?

PERFECTION. No. I actually….

HUNGER. Had an entire pecan pie, a dozen plain cake donuts, a chili dog with sauerkraut and extra onions and cheese, five Tweenkies, a liter bottle of Liebfraumilch, while riding the Lazy-Boy's massage feature on high?

PERFECTION. No. No. A small dose of cough medicine, so I could sleep. I…I fear that's why he can't spell rhododendron.

(*Beat.* **MOTHER PERFECTION** *fights back tears as* **MOTHER DESIRE** *and* **MOTHER HUNGER** *attempt to spell rhododendron – neither are able to.*)

HUNGER. Three-year-olds can spell rhododendron, but so what? What good is spelling if you can't physically dominate your opponent and take what you want at will? Because if you don't they will.

DESIRE. Exactly. So what if they're only fourth graders? Eventually they're going to be competing for the same executive position and the only way they're going to succeed then and there is by kicking some ass out there.

HUNGER. Bill! Bill, go for a headlock then, transfer immediately to the sleeper hold and then….

DESIRE. Jeremy, just kick! Just drop your head and kick wildly like a crazed and cornered Wildebeest.

PERFECTION. I'm sorry, ladies, but I cannot condone such outrageous behavior, nor your acceptance of it. Alexander! Alexander, I grant you permission to retaliate – but only within the boundaries as outlined and prescribed by the ethicist Ashanti Shantar.

*(*MOTHER DESIRE *and* MOTHER HUNGER *react.*
MOTHER PERFECTION *remains unmoved. Once the
"battle" is over* MOTHER PERFECTION *returns to her
previous position.)*

PERFECTION. Perhaps fourth graders should only be concerned with soccer and not executive positions?

HUNGER. Ma'am, I must confess your child's display was impeccable – Billy's broken nose and clavicle could not have been more perfectly administered.

DESIRE. And I too will admit it was incredible. Jeremy can't help but learn something from his compound fractured tibia. Alexander possesses both agility and strength with a clear capacity to unleash just retribution. Madame I commend you.

HUNGER. Surely, you visited the Harmenlicktensteinenlagendarmenglaberschpeil Institute for their inter-utero injection of sterile sheep venom?

DESIRE. Perhaps you traveled to El Santiago high in the Andes and, during a full moon in late spring, drank from the rough and worn stone blood troughs of the Incas?

PERFECTION. Ladies, I'm sorry, but your speculations are ill-founded. Once impregnated by his father....

HUNGER. Who'd been drinking the WWF analgesic bodybuilding laxative RRFGTH-23 and....

DESIRE. ...And receiving hair, calf, peck, and thigh implants while undergoing nuclear metabolic stimulation from a team of Russian meta-scientists....

HUNGER. ...Who'd distilled a dark elixir from the mummified remains of an Egyptian wooly mammoth....

DESIRE. ...That'd been discovered down river from Chernobyl....

PERFECTION. No. No. No. And, double-plus No squaredinfinitely. I ate sensibly, slept soundly and deeply, and exercised regularly, but moderately.

DESIRE/HUNGER. What?!

HUNGER. You are perverse.

DESIRE. But you read to him while he was inside?

PERFECTION. Occasionally…But only the classics.

HUNGER. Perverse.

DESIRE. What about leather straps, cattle prods, and water depravation?

PERFECTION. Excuse me?

DESIRE. Well, not while inside, but…surely you used wooden spoons and pellet guns to keep him from crawling all over and coloring on the walls?

PERFECTION. I'm sorry, but…am I in some strange nightmare?

DESIRE. The real question is why do you go to such extremes without rhyme or reason?

PERFECTION. Why do I….?

HUNGER. Yes. To what end do you spoil him like some King of Kings?

PERFECTION. Spoil? I only give him….

HUNGER. Don't lie. Just the other day I saw you purchase underwear for him.

DESIRE. Perhaps you hope he connives himself into some political office where the secretaries are easy and the power is bountiful?

HUNGER. Maybe become some exalted sports celebrity where the cheerleaders are easy and the power is bountiful?

PERFECTION. I hope he's happy and content regardless where and what he does.

DESIRE. Liar!

HUNGER. Blasphemer!

PERFECTION. Alexander, it's time to leave. Freaks abound and infiltrate this suddenly strange land. Let us seek refuge.

*(***MOTHER DESIRE*** and ***MOTHER HUNGER*** grab and hold ***MOTHER PERFECTION****.)*

DESIRE. Little lady, you best tell us your intricately articulate plans for his life, lest you force me to get my cattle prod.

HUNGER. Or I begin tweaking your thumbs up to your elbow. Now talk.

PERFECTION. Honestly, there are no plans, there's only hope for his happiness.

(**MOTHER DESIRE** and **MOTHER HUNGER** begin to torture **MOTHER PERFECTION**.)

HUNGER. Cough it up, or your thumb pops out.

PERFECTION. Okay. Okay. I'll talk. I'll talk.

HUNGER. And who says force doesn't lead to truth? Now share your sweet, dark secret vixen.

PERFECTION. He's going to be a saint.

DESIRE. Uh…a what?

HUNGER. Why…why do you want him to live in Missouri?

DESIRE. I thought they were in Louisiana? Maybe New Orleans?

PERFECTION. He's going to be a non-denominational savior. He's going to be a gleaming example of how to live a pristine and meaningful life, without the twisted deprecation of asceticism, fanaticism, or daytime television.

DESIRE. Yeah, and I'm Oprah frigging Winfrey. There's no way to get a saint these days without a soundproof room and a cattle prod.

PERFECTION. I wash his clothes in purified water from Fiji. He only wears natural fabrics sewn by blind virgins.

HUNGER. So, that explains his uniform.

PERFECTION. He's memorized all the religious texts in the world – even Dianetics. He speaks twenty languages – fluently. When he's not volunteering at the homeless leper shelter he's assisting migrant workers with….

DESIRE. Okay, okay. He's a friggin' saint at eight. Big deal.

HUNGER. Yeah, great future digging wells in some Third World piss hole, while scratching mosquito bites raw.

DESIRE. Exactly. And our sons? Ours will be penthouse, Porsche, and Perrier-Jouet success stories from the impeccable laws of simple, sweet natural selection.

HUNGER. Right. The strong shall survive, and will conquer, and, therefore, wear expensive suits made by poor children in poor countries.

PERFECTION. I wonder who will be making suits for those children when they convert to Alexanderianism and take over the world?

DESIRE. Is that in Georgia?

HUNGER. He's...he's going to start a...a religion?

PERFECTION. Yes. There will be thick books with thin truths. Long hours on satellite television. Marches and crusades. Concerts and cotillions. And everything will have monthly dues and entrance fees. Praise Alexander. Praise – say it with me – Praise Alexander.

HUNGER. He'll...he'll be famous. Make millions, billions, trillions. Be seen everywhere by everyone. You asshole.

DESIRE. Yes, yes, he will. What assholes.

HUNGER. They'll sell shirts, coffee mugs, mouse pads, candles, coasters, caps, calendars....

DESIRE. It's...it's brilliant.

HUNGER. ...Pens, key chains, dinner plates, sweatshirts....

PERFECTION. Yes, it is. And you and your Cro-Magnon clan of nincompoops can keep your penthouses and Porsches. I want Paris, Peking and Pakistan. And, by sacred Alexander, I shall have them. Now, ladies, good day. And, as the Sumatrans say, erba numa bertala gur aba nu – "eat tapir dung and like it." Again, good day.

(**MOTHER PERFECTION** *exits.* **MOTHER HUNGER** *and* **MOTHER DESIRE** *stand perplexed. Beat.*)

DESIRE. Is...is it wrong to...to kind of admire her?

HUNGER. No. But...but I fear....

DESIRE. I...I do too.

HUNGER. I fear were too far behind to catch them.

DESIRE. Speak for yourself. Like I said, cattle prod, sander, and a soundproof room. Jeremy, I'll meet you at the car. I don't care. You've still got one good leg and two strong arms. Just do it.

(again with the cattle prod and sander)

Do it. Do it. Besides mama can't carry you, she's gotta pee.

*(**MOTHER DESIRE** exits.)*

HUNGER. Billy? Billy, I...I know what I said about blow jobs and meaningless sex, and that won't change, don't get me wrong, but instead of luxury items and Paris Hilton prostitutes, what about taking over the world? Yes, the whole thing. Slowly, one mind at a time. Everyone's. More than likely there will be lots of blood. Yes, you'll like that, won't you? That's my boy. Well, I think, for a starter we might cut your hair. It won't be that bad. No, no it won't. Honest, you can trust your mother.

(Lights slowly fade to black.)

End

PROPERTY LIST

TONGUE, TIED
Couch
Hand puppets (4)

DEATH AND JAVIER MIGUEL LOPES GUADALAJARA
Portable espresso cart
Broom
Dust pan
Trashcan on wheels
Energy drink

CLOWNS
Pint bottle
Paper bag
Flute

SKIRMISHES
A breadcrumb (large)
Picnic basket
Miscellaneous picnic items
Binoculars (2)

THE PLAID MAN
Table
Chairs (2)
Wine bottle
Wine glasses (2)

NORTH POLE WINTER WOES
Bar
Miscellaneous bottles
Stools (2)
Eye glasses

THE ABDUCTION
Portable lounge chairs (2)
Cooler
Fifth of tequila
Beer cans

NATURAL SELECTION

From Reviews and Testimonials of
TONGUE, TIED AND OTHER SHORT PLAYS...

"This one's definitely a comedy, and a bit raucous too."
– Joel Pierson

"...the mesmerizing, very funny *Tongue, Tied...*"
- Judith Egerton, *Louisville's Courier-Journal*

OTHER TITLES AVAILABLE FROM SAMUEL FRENCH

TREASURE ISLAND
Ken Ludwig

All Groups / Adventure / 10m, 1f (doubling) / Areas
Based on the masterful adventure novel by Robert Louis Stevenson, *Treasure Island* is a stunning yarn of piracy on the tropical seas. It begins at an inn on the Devon coast of England in 1775 and quickly becomes an unforgettable tale of treachery and mayhem featuring a host of legendary swashbucklers including the dangerous Billy Bones (played unforgettably in the movies by Lionel Barrymore), the sinister two-timing Israel Hands, the brassy woman pirate Anne Bonney, and the hideous form of evil incarnate, Blind Pew. At the center of it all are Jim Hawkins, a 14-year-old boy who longs for adventure, and the infamous Long John Silver, who is a complex study of good and evil, perhaps the most famous hero-villain of all time. Silver is an unscrupulous buccaneer-rogue whose greedy quest for gold, coupled with his affection for Jim, cannot help but win the heart of every soul who has ever longed for romance, treasure and adventure.

OTHER TITLES AVAILABLE FROM SAMUEL FRENCH

THREE MUSKETEERS
Ken Ludwig

All Groups / Adventure / 8m, 4f (doubling) / Unit sets
This adaptation is based on the timeless swashbuckler by Alexandre Dumas, a tale of heroism, treachery, close escapes and above all, honor. The story, set in 1625, begins with d'Artagnan who sets off for Paris in search of adventure. Along with d'Artagnan goes Sabine, his sister, the quintessential tomboy. Sent with d'Artagnan to attend a convent school in Paris, she poses as a young man – d'Artagnan's servant – and quickly becomes entangled in her brother's adventures. Soon after reaching Paris, d'Artagnan encounters the greatest heroes of the day, Athos, Porthos and Aramis, the famous musketeers; d'Artagnan joins forces with his heroes to defend the honor of the Queen of France. In so doing, he finds himself in opposition to the most dangerous man in Europe, Cardinal Richelieu. Even more deadly is the infamous Countess de Winter, known as Milady, who will stop at nothing to revenge herself on d'Artagnan – and Sabine – for their meddlesome behavior. Little does Milady know that the young girl she scorns, Sabine, will ultimately save the day.